Bakhtin's Carnival

LAOMA's three kinds of dramas

LAOMA

KR International Business

Bakhtin's Carnival

LaoMa
Chinese Edition Copyright : 2012 by China Renmin University Press

ISBN: 978-981-09-3378-4

Published by
KR International Business
12 Holland Avenue #22-35,Singapore272012

Publication Date:May25,2015
Publisher: KR International Business
Language: English
Trim Size: 7"x10"
Page Count: 149

Bakhtin's Carnival

LAOMA's three kinds of dramas

1. Bakhtin's carnival

2. Socrates

3. Svejk

The creation of Matt Marko's dramas did not focus on how to organize the fierce and intense conflict, but to imply special situation of the era by means of the comedy content.

Content

Bakhtin's carnival 05

Carnival laughter is a unique humor of the festival. It is not the individual response to a simple and laughable phenomenon.

Socrates 42

As long as I have life and ability, I will never stop practicing the philosophy, to clarify the truth to everyone I met.

Svejk 97

The era was enlightened now. If, in the first few years, to say this sentence, you would sentence to ten years in jail again, or perhaps directly hanged. The emperor who was ate up by the rats had more serious sins than the one whose body was covered with the excrement of the flies!

Bakhtin's Carnival

Characters

Bakhtin: a famous philosopher and humanities scholars in the former Soviet Union, and one of the world's most important thinkers in the 20th century. He was sentenced and banished for the lectures in a small private gathering in his youth, then served as university professor. Since the 1960s, he has always played a significant influence on philosophy, literature, aesthetics, poetics, linguistics, semiotics, history and culture, and other fields.

Yelina: Bakhtin's wife.

Rabelais: a novelist, who was one of the representatives of the French Renaissance in the 16th century, and served as a doctor, wrote the novel "Giant" handed down.

Gao-lang Gujie: a character in the Rabelais' "Giant", who was the father of Gragantua.

Gragantua: the hero in the Rabelais' "Giant", a giant.

Pantagruel: one of the leading characters in the Rabelais "Giant", the son of Gragantua

Douay: the character in the Rabelais "Giant", a judge.

Baiz Gyl: the character in the Rabelais "Giant", a milord.

Yu-Mo Weyna: the character in the Rabelais "Giant", a milord.

Landlady, police A, police B. King, judges, lawyers, bishops, servants, the chairman of the dissertation committee, oral defense committee professors (four), two scorers, the professors of the classroom discussion, a dozen students.

"Act I"

(A room for sleeping and study. The simple furniture: a single bed and a desk. Piles of books are put on the floor and the desk. Bakhtin is lying on the desk to write.)

(Landlady appears on the scene. She stretches her dress and apron, and deliberately coughs twice.)

Landlady: Excuse me, Mr. Bakhtin. I have to interrupt your work, if you stay in the house all day long, which is also called the work.

Bakhtin: Oh, my dear landlady, hi! Your coming just makes my brain rapidly running temporarily rest. I am really at work, and not lazy. This work is somewhat different from the intensive labor in factories and workshops and the collective farm, but actually they are the same.

Landlady: Mr. Bakhtin, I'm so happy to hear that. Now that you stay in the house every day to work, you must have a fixed salary like workers in the factory, then please you pay the rent in arrears to me.

Bakhtin: I'm sorry, landlady. Please give me a few days again. As long as my paper is issued, I will get royalties. All the rent will be paid to you as soon as I get the royalties.

Landlady: I am more embarrassed, Mr. Bakhtin. Two months ago, I seemed to hear you say the same words, and a month ago, it seemed that you also said so.

Bakhtin: Landlady, in fact, you know, I have always receive the rejection from the editorial department in a few months, rather than royalties ......

Landlady: Are you sure that you can not receive the rejection this month?

Bakhtin: I promise you, my paper must be published this time.

Because I borrowed a friend's name, regarded him as the author of the paper, which is more reliable and easier to escape the review of higher authorities than my name Bakhtin.

Landlady: Oh, my god! What a pity, Mr. Bakhtin! Why do not you go to openly participate in collective labor, and to earn a decent wage, instead of surreptitiously writing these papers that nobody would like to need like thieves? I do not really understand, your body seems to be able to carry shovels and axes, can't you go to build the railway or serve as a lumberjack?

Bakhtin: Landlady, the world's people do not have to be engaged in the same profession. My brain is more valuable than the limbs, filled with philosophy, literature, anthropology, aesthetics, semiotics, linguistics and other strange ideas, I think about these issues, and to tell the conclusions to people, which is a labor, not less than the contribution of the manual workers to build railways or lumber.

Illustrator: Gustave Dore

Landlady: Mr. Bakhtin, maybe you're right, but I do not care what your contribution, and I just want to take back a little rent that I deserve, if you do not take it out today, I have to ask you to move elsewhere to think. Please forgive me, I have to do this, you also have to understand my difficulties!

Bakhtin :(circling back and forth in the house, rubbing his hands, he can find no way out .) Landlady, for the sake of god, please give[3] me a few days again.

Landlady: There is not God in the world at all. Please do not use it as pledge!

Bakhtin: Stay two days again, alright ? Tomorrow is Christmas. (Two policemen come on the stage.)

Police A: No! You must go with us right now!

Bakhtin: (Looking at the landlady) For this little thing, you also want to disturb the police?

Landlady: (In a panic) No, no, no! You must misunderstand, Mr. Bakhtin, I did not alarm!

Police B: You are the landlady?

Landlady: Yes. What did he commit ? I only rented the house to him, and I do not know nothing about what he actually did!

Police A: Why do you stand here?

Landlady: I was about to make him go away, and he has held off for three months of rent!

Police B: That do not bother you again, and we will help him find a place to live. Come on, Mr. Bakhtin, I promise you need not pay for there!

Bakhtin: What are you doing? Where do you want to take me?

Police A: Don't you see what we are doing? Can't you see we wear these clothes? Haha, no wonder some people said "you're a nerd"! Come on, you have no place to live just now, and we have arranged a room for you in prison.

Bakhtin: Prison? Why let me go there? I did not murder, commit arson, and not steal, rob!

Police B: The crime does not refer to murder, arson, theft or robbery, some crimes may be more subtle, more dangerous. Some people have nothing to do, and there are always some thoughts to appear in their brains, to secretly laugh at our social system. For example, like you ...... what was it called?

Police A: Intellectuals!

Police B: Yes, intellectuals! The name is very strange, it seems that only you have the knowledge, do not the police like us, as well as workers, farmers have no knowledge?

Bakhtin: No, no, no, my policemen, the intellectuals do not mean what you understand!

Police B: Look, look, I made a mistake again, and not even understand what the intellectuals are. Mr. Bakhtin, do you want to say we are very stupid?

Bakhtin: No, no, no, I did not mean ......

Police A: What do you mean?

Bakhtin: I mean ......

Police A: There is no meaning if you say again! Do you know why we have to arrest you?

Bakhtin: I do not know.

Police A: Shit! You are really able to show, with a look of innocence, like a scapegoat! I ask you, have you held some activities such as salon or lecture at home these years?

Bakhtin: Yes, occasionally there are five or six young scholars to get together to discuss issues of common interest.

Police B: What about?

Illustrator: Gustave Dore

Bakhtin: They are purely academic issues about German classical philosophy and modern philosophy, such as Kant, Husserl, Schuller, also involving Freud's views ......

Police B: Why do not you seriously study and publicize Leninism and Stalin's thought? Why not to actively participate in collective productive labor of Soviet socialism?

Bakhtin: This...... my policeman, because I am suffering from osteomyelitis, and other diseases, only to stay at home and in bed, so that I lost the possibility of engaging in any other manual labor, which is the most important reason. But I'm loyal to the Soviet regime, and interested in Marxism......

Police A: Haha, it seems that osteomyelitis has invaded your brain. Without the approval of their superior, you organize what is called study groups in your family, to spread some bad idea. Is it not illegal yet?

Bakhtin: But….. I did not oppose to the Soviets, on the contrary, I have been......

Police A: Mr. Bakhtin, please do not quibble for yourself. (Take out a piece of paper from his jacket pocket) Now I pronounced on behalf of the State Security Department: "Mikhail Bakhtin • Mikhailovich, 33 years old, married, son of a bank clerk, a university degree, claimed to be Marxist. According to the investigation, the prisoner has always stayed at home in the name of losing the ability to work, illegally gathering others, and holding the so-called academic discussion and lecture with anti-soviet thinking, which has constituted the crime of subverting the Soviet regime. Hereby arrest you and sentence to hard labor and five years of living in prison. Immediate execution. "

Bakhtin: I did not carry out the illegal activities! Subjectively speaking, the academic research that I have been engaged in did not pursue any political goals against the Soviet Union.

Police B: We think you are illegal, you are illegal! It can not follow your own desires.

Bakhtin: My god, today is Christmas Eve, and tomorrow is Christmas, why can it happen this time?

Police A: Look, your brain is full of religious superstition, and you also want to choose a good time to go to jail, God and Christ can not save you now!

Bakhtin : (Shouting at the landlady directly) Landlady, please tell my wife Yelina I was taken away, let her find someone to save me!

Landlady: I heard you, Mr. Bakhtin, I'll tell her. You take care of yourself! (wiping her tears and sighing) Oh, I failed to get my rent again.

Police B: Take away all of the manuscripts you wrote, these are the evidences! Bakhtin: (Taken away by two police officers, he turned back and shouted) Your rent I owned to you will be paid for you by my wife!

"End"

"**Act Ⅱ**"

(Kostanay, which is the penal colony. Bakhtin and his wife Yelina sat in a corner of the stage.)

Bakhtin: Yelina, I make you suffer. If my business did not get you in trouble, you would not be exiled to this uninhabited wilderness, to suffer from the humiliation and tough live. Darling, all the misfortunes are caused by me.

Yelina: Honey, please do not say that. Just to be with you, I will feel happy and warm. I have nothing to complain that, even my heart is often filled with gratitude to God. Of course, we also thank Ms. Gao Erji. Without her help and pleading, you would be still held in prison. The exile is much better that imprisonment, at least I'm by your side.

Bakhtin: Yes, my dear wife. You accompany me, I am always burning. Look, how bright the stars, we seem to be in heaven.

Yelina: The stars here are very close to us, as if we can reach them with hands. In St. Petersburg and Moscow, we can not see this amazing sight!

Bakhtin: Yes, the sky is full of gray there, stars are no longer flashing, the sky is pale, and the earth keeps silent ......

Yelina: Hush! Keep a low voice, honey, don't make others hear.

Bakhtin: (Sigh) Well ...... (deep in thought)

Yelina: Honey, what are you thinking?

Bakhtin: Happy and noisy scenes and witty stories often appear in my mind, depicted in the novel "Giant" by French writer Rabelais[3].......

Yelina: Really? Tell it to me.

Bakhtin: Okay, honey. Five hundred years ago, a monk, whose pseudonym was Rabelais, wrote a novel, there are many funny

and humorous, absurd and amusing stories in the book, full
of happiness and cynicism. For example, the carnival on the
street square......
(The follow lighting on Bakhtin and Yelina's heads turns dark,
and the center of the stage turns bright. Carnival is ongoing.
Laughing, singing and shouting are mixed together.)
Gao-lang Gujie: To drink, drink! To celebrate the birth of
Gragantua's son, we enjoy drinking! Come on, give me a big
bucket, this glass is too small, I want to drain the Pacific
Ocean!
A: I'm the King. Come on, fill my glass with the red wine!
B: Hey, Your Majesty, you are a little fly in the nude, a bug
stained with rats' excrement, you want to drink red wine? No!
Can I give you a large glass of yellow wine? Come on, cheers,
alright? This is the horse urine, from an old mare catching
up with venereal disease!
A: Shit! You dare to take the horse urine to fool me, why not
to give me donkey urine?
B: My foolish King, the donkey urine has been poured into his
stomach by the bishop who is more stupid than you.
A: Let him drink, the one who has loose bowels need not worry
about shit. I swear to God's navel that the bishop is just
a nagging, whining coward, just a fly with green head buzzing
around the dunghill!
C: Your Majesty, you are finally correct. The bishop's wear
always incurs the world's contempt and cursing, because they
live on human beings' sins, so religious people are called
the men eating shit. We should put them thrown into the garbage
and manure pit, namely, the monasteries and churches, making
them isolated, as the toilet must be separated from the house.

A: What fuck you? You are only a wildcat wearing a robe of fur! Your Honor, you know nothing about the law in addition to corruption through misuse of law, bribe and extortion. Do you know that the law is a spider web, which can only capture the civilians like gadfly, but without any constraints for powerful officials and lords. You do not deserve to wear the "sanctimonious" robe.

C: Your Majesty, you have been covered with feces, but detest others. I want to publicly take off your crown, take off your pants and let everybody look at whether your noble body is also covered with arteries and veins and boils!

Gao-lang Gujie: Keep silent! Today is my son's birthday of five years old, everybody should enjoy drinking. I tell you, my famous friends, if you do not drink in your life, you will be worse than a dog! When my son was born from the womb, he shouted: "Drink, drink, drink!" So I named him Gargantua, meaning "so big throat!" Give him a drink every day. This kid's capacity for alcohol is surprising, drinking wine more than milk! As long as drinking wine enough, he does not lose his temper and cry any more. He does not like any toys, only willing to play with barrels, wine glasses and bottles.

A: I have heard that this great little guy is drinking in addition to eating all day; or drink and eat, drink and sleep. He also farted in the oil, peed towards the sun, hid in the water to get out of the rain, and tickled himself, ate cabbage but discharge leeks, urinary bladder as the lantern, cloud as the quilt, pull out the legs of flies, and kiss the mouth of the mosquito, so insane!

Gao-lang Gujie: Haha, you, a rascal king, incompetent and

decadent, shit on the people's head, dared compliment my baby son in so nasty tone under the large crowd. You know, my son is a genius, and his birth is a miracle in itself. His mother, that is, my dear wife Jia Jia Meli, during her pregnancy, particularly like to eat cow intestines, during this period, I killed three hundred sixty-seven thousand and fourteen strong cattle, she ate all the intestines. Before she was in labor, I persuaded her, it was bad for her to eat the stuff, because in a sense to eat the intestines is to eat feces. But she was too greedy, so that she ate a hearty meal again, as a result, the anus dropped, and nearly suffocated my son.

B: Yes, I was in childbirth scene and witnessed the thrilling scene. I called the midwife, and gave her to take restringent medicine with strong effect. I did not expect Jiajia Meli shrunk suddenly, the foreskin of her placenta was broken. The baby suddenly jumped up from the womb, got into the artery, through the diaphragm of her heart, climbed to the left shoulder, and finally drilled out from his mother's left ear. Haha, how dangerous!

Gao-liang Gujie: Look, my son is coming, only five years old, how strong he is!

(Gargantua appears)

Gargantua: (carrying wine pot in his hands towards Gao-lang Gu Jie) Dad, have a drink! (Hold up the pot, "Codoon, Codoon", drink)

Gao-lang Gujie: Look, my son has not only great capacity for liquor, but high IQ, and approachable as well. He never regards me as an outsider, especially in front of guests, always think of me as his own brother, and never put on airs. Come on, my little baby, to accompany your father, you have another drink!

Gargantua:(drained, wiping his mouth) My father as the brother, the wine all-pervasive in my whole body, quench my thirst very much.

Gao-lang Gujie: My son, this wine is on my appetite, we should knock at barrels to tell everybody, the one who does not want to drink in the world do not deserve to live.

D:(Bishop) This is God saying, nobody likes to drink beyond me as bishop's messenger of God. Gargantua, I ask you, how to deal with thirst?

Gargantua: Opposite to preventing the dog. If running behind the dog, you can not be bit by the dog; If drinking before thirsty, you will never be thirsty again.

D: Exactly, my smartest kid. Don't drink when you are thirsty, do not eat when you are hungry, you should drink and eat in advance, and you feel never hungry and thirsty. Come on, wine! I want to make a new record. I want a big cup!

Gargantua:(Take off the giant shoes) My shoe is big enough, and you use it to drink!

Gao-lang Gujie: You can not do that, my son! Bishop's mouth is dirty, he will make shoe dirty!

Gargantua: This shoe has just stepped on the shit, it is a very appropriate glass for the father.

Gao-lang Gujie: If so, give the shoe to the king!

Gargantua: Up to my father. Come on, (pour out some liquor into shoe) I have a toast to my king!

A: Thank you, happy birthday and good health! I drink a toast! (Wipe his mouth) Wow, this white wine tastes good, as soft as silk! Look, even the flies like to drink, I invite the flies to drink with me!

All :(raising their glasses and shout loudly) Cheers! Cheers!

Cheers!

Illustrator: Gustave Dore

(Lights turn dark. The follow lighting hits Bakhtin and his wife in the corner of the stage.)

Bakhtin: Honey, Yelina, look, the carnival written by Rabelais is such a scene, the people were allowed in the festival to gather in the square, happily drinking, drinking and eating, without any constraints, the original order was disrupted, reversed, the king, bishops, judges and other dignitaries were in derision, tricked, while civilians became giants, unrestrained and indulgence ......

Yelina: But, honey, their language is vulgar, and even ...... I mean, their bad language make me feel uncomfortable a little.

Bakhtin: Yes, I can understand how you feel. Square's language was so vulgar those days, even dirty, full of insults and curses, so that our ears can not accept. However, so vulgar language had the strong force on the comical adaptation, derogation, materialization and embodiments of the world. They are both traditional and widely popular. Rabelais deliberately used the absolutely cheerful, fearless, unrestrained and straightforward and frank words to fiercely fire to the " Gothic dark ". You can listen to what Rabelais said.

(It is Rabelais' turn. Follow lighting moves to him.)

Rabelais: Dear, readers and viewers, as well as those who I do not like friends have nothing to do but to simply make money, serve as officials struggling for power, when you read the name of a few books I wrote, like "Gargantua "" Pantagruel "," Drinker "," Crotch dignity ", and so forth, you will assume that the book is nothing but hip-hop jokes and nonsense. In fact, this is just a pretext. If not delve into them, you will really regard these books as funny and superficial works like games. Oh, you know, there is not good wine in a beautiful bottle, and treasures may be found in the tattered box; the one wearing the cassock is not monk, and the monk does not necessarily recite scriptures; the one wearing the cloak is not necessarily a knight, and not all the knights are brave. Not winded, and you knock on their bones to suck the fresh and fragrant marrow. Whether religion or political situation and economic life, my works will give you extremely profound and divine philosophy and intriguing mystery! This work is finished using the time of drinking and eating, filled with meat and wine taste, as long as you boast I am a master of jokes, I would feel very honor and glory.

Now, my dear friends, happily go on reading it. I hope you feel comfortable, and relax limbs! When you go back, do not forget to have a toast for me, I promise to retaliate you immediately!

"End"

"Act Ⅲ"

(The scene is similar to the previous. Gargantua appears on the scene.)

Gargantua: I am Gargantua, the descendant of the giant. You just saw what I look like when I was five years old, and now I am more than nine years old. Time flies too fast. It is not long time to call others Grandpa, I was called grandpa by others. My father Gao-lang Gujie has passed away, and I am an orphan now. Fortunately, in my four hundred eighty plus 44, my wife Bud Baker princess gave birth to a lovely son for me, called Pantagruel.

Servant: Yes, his son is like him as a child, unrestrained to drink and eat, and powerful. In the womb all the teeth came out, He drank milk from of four thousand six hundred cow when born, and even milk buckets were swallowed into him stomach. A big black bear came to lick milk on his lips, and he caught the big bear immediately, tore it like a chicken, and then ate it as snacks.

Gargantua: This child is too fat, and too strong, if his mother did not stifle, he could not be born at all. Alas, my beloved wife died, I was very sad, and my son was born, I'm very happy. At that time, I do not really know what to do, should I cry for my wife dead, or delight for newborn son? I thought repeatedly, thinking over and over again, finally decided to cry before laugh. I cried very seriously, and laughed happily.

Servant: Pantagruel became a poor little child losing mother when he was born, his father Gargantua is both his father and mother, extremely worry about his son.

Gargantua: Well, a strict father can teach his son well. The education of the son is every father's bounden duty. When my son Pantagruel studied in law school, he was always afraid that his studies made his brain and eyes tired, so he often danced, played tennis. He said: "the ball is in the trousers' pocket, and the racket is in hand. The tie is on behalf of legal knowledge, and their heels can show dancing skills, which are the marks of JD. Now my son Pantagruel has been already a well-known master of the law, judges, lawyers, experts and professors have to consult Pantagruel when they meet difficult problems on litigation, so wherever he goes, there are always groups of people to follow behind him for advice! Look, he is coming! I do not want to delay his valuable time, and not greet him! Let's go! (Call his servant.) We go around elsewhere.

(Pantagruel comes on the stage, followed by seven or eight men.)

Douay: Dear, Master Pantagruel, please stop, and just give me a few minutes. I know you are very busy, but the case with which we are faced is very, very difficult, and very, very complicated, very, very hard to deal with it. We admire your knowledge very much, please you must take time out from your busy schedule to give some advice to us.

Pantagruel:(Stopped) Is there so much "very, very" in the world? Okay, tell me, what lawsuit is that on earth?

Douay: This is..[3]....

Lawyer: (take up the subject of the conversation) Let me tell you, because I understand the whole proceedings.

Pantagruel: Well, you have to be concise.

Lawyer: Yes, master Pantagruel, this is my strength. When I

was a child, the third uncle's wife of my mother's second aunt praised me, "when this kid tells the story, his logic is clear and his language is concise, etc.."

Pantagruel: Wait, wait! Please start with the case, and stay on point, as for how your aunts praised you, you set it aside!

Lawyer: Okay, Okay, Okay! It is that there are two great men, the one is the plaintiff Baiz Gyl, the other is the defendant Yu-Mo Weyna. From a legal point of view this litigation between them is so profound, so complex, so strange, so strange, and so so, the Supreme Court simply become increasingly confused. Finally, in accordance with the king's decree, convened four most knowledgeable, renowned experts recognized nationally in the legal profession, in conjunction with the Supreme Court, the famous professors from various universities, except France, hired a lot of legal authorities from the United Kingdom, Italy and other countries. They were sleepless nights together and have studied this case for the forty-six weeks, spending a lot of money, but failed to find any clues, while all the judges, professors and jurists involved in the case were very, very embarrassed, and many people shit because of shame. This is a great shame and heavy burden conscientiously for us. Therefore, we urge you to express and give us direction.

Pantagruel: You ask me for expressing what, pointing where? How about the case in the end, you said it for a long time, but not speak of any clues about it.

Lawyer: As for details of the case, I can't really make it clear, and nobody can do it. If the case can be understood clearly, we would not have to trouble you!

Douay: Yes, master. All dossiers of this case are complete, including their statements, arguments and relevant evidences, etc., and the whole room has been filled with them. We can first carry a batch using a carriage, please have a look.

Pantagruel: Is it useful to read a pile of paper? Why not call the parties, and let them state and debate face to face! Go, call two men having dispute to come here immediately!

 (Two old men come on the stage.)

Two men:(unison) Hi, Master!

Pantagruel: This case is about both you?

Two men: Yes, sir.

Pantagruel: Which one is the plaintiff?

Baiz Gyl: It's me.

Pantagruel: Well, my friend, at this moment you have to face the crowd and me to state this case concretely again. God is looking at us, if you talk one word irresponsibly, I will cut off your head from your shoulders. I want to tell you, in the presence of justice, you can only tell the truth, and not lie. So, you have to be careful especially, what you said can be neither exaggerated, nor reduced. Now, you can start.

Baiz Gyl: Master, it was actually like this, (take out a piece of paper from a hat) the clue is very clear! An old woman from my home sold eggs in the woods......

Pantagruel: Give him a chair. You can sit down to say.

Baiz Gyl:(Sit down) Thank you, master! At that time, six pieces of silver and one cup flew towards the zenith from Erzhixian. That year happened to be the absence of hypocritical fraud on Liffey hill,[3] so that the provocative rumors about Switzerland rebel were caused by two religious sects of rubbish and nonsense. The number of these Swiss gathered was 3690, in order that on the day of the New Year they can use soup to feed cows, and give the coal key to the little girl

and tell her to use the bread to carry the wood...... Through
a night, hands puts on the kettle, only want to ride on the
ship, because the tailor intends to use the rags stolen to
do a barrel and then defends the oceans, according to a man
bundling, the ocean is pregnant because of a pot of cabbage
soup, but doctors says there are no signs of the outbreak of
war, judging from the urine. From the posture of ducks walking,
I can't see how to eat the spade with the mustard, unless
forensic lords give syphilis a low chromatic command that they
are not allowed to focus on the men to sell pot again, because
those poor guys are dancing in accordance with the beats, one
foot on the fire, head in the crotch, already busy enough.
Haha, gentlemen, Gods, according to their own wills,
constraint all things. Coachman makes the whip broken, and
the judge has to circle to lick his fingers with goose feather,
at least, but not release the bird without seeing the cake.
Since the anti-shoe is often worn, often no memory. God blesses
Mitana!
Pantagruel: Very good, friend, very good! Slow down, do not
worry! Your logic is clear, keep going.
Yu-Mo Weyna : (defendant): Master, master, I want to say.
Pantagruel: Shut up! Nobody allows you to speak, you do not
interrupt. What the plaintiff said is so good, you can speak
when he finishes, and I promise to give you time enough to
say !
Illustrator: Wen³-Zhe Ma
Baiz Gyl: The pope has allowed everyone to fart at random,
only the white cloth is still not painted, no matter how poor
the world is, they do not use the left hand to paint the cross,
hatch eggs or build the rainbow for the jackass, that woman

is allowed to neglect protests of the small goldfish with testis, because of the small goldfish is a tool that must be used to repair the old boots, so there are a particularly large number of snails this year, you can unlock the buttons on the stomach. Master, for this reason, I ask the defendant to compensate all losses, including interest. Please master upholds justice!

Pantagruel: So you do not have anything else to say it?

Baiz Gyl: No, master. I swore by my honor the bird can't keep shitting!

Pantagruel: So, now it is the defendant Mr. Yu-Mo Weyna's turn. You should try to speak concisely, but do not miss the useful details.

Yu-Mo Weyna: Master and gentlemen, if the injustice of the world can be identified as clearly as a fly in the milk, then the world would not have been bitten by mice like this. The plaintiff's statement is really as seamless as the velvet. Ah, the Virgin! We have seen tall officers stand on the battlefield to fart loudly, and now even the super woolen goods has not been gotten, and if the court does not order, then this year's ethos of the robbery will be as serious as drinking in the past and the future. It is assumed that a sufferer wipes his mouth with cow dung in the bath house, then all living things will fall into darkness. At the age of thirty six, I bought a German horse, and I'm not so knowledgeable, to use the teeth to bite[3] the moon. Some people said that eating the corned beef, wine can still be found in the night without candles. As the saying goes, the black cow burned is also visible when you enjoy love. Gentlemen, do not believe in that woman. Of course, the cow involved had not a good memory. I'm sure, with six-silver coins, you can buy all the wool in the market, because as long as a suit of armor has the taste of garlic, the internal liver was eroded by the rust. The one who was the first to fire will wipe the snot when singing. No other words, I claim the compensation of costs, losses and interest.

Pantagruel: The plaintiff has anything to plead?

Baiz Gyl: No, master, because every word I said is the truth, for the stake of God, please settle the dispute between us, we both spent too much on the litigation!

Pantagruel: Well, judges, scholars, professors and experts, you have heard their statement, how you think?

The others:(unison) Yes, we all heard. But, we understand nothing.

Pantagruel: let them re-say it again!

The others: No! We urge master to sentence it rightly, and absolutely agree. Everyone is in favor!

Pantagruel :(turn twice in situ, slightly pensive) Well, thank you for your trust, now I solemnly pronounce: Because of bats' impulsion, they left the Tropic of Cancer boldly to pursue boring game, but because they are afraid of the sun, pawns attacked firstly, this is the weather in Rome, a status of Jesus on a horse, with a bow hung on his waist, the plaintiff has a legitimate reason to repair fishing boats. The old woman was ordered to wear one shoe, and the other foot was bare, blown, her conscience became strong and hard, and trivial things, as many as the hair of eighteen cattle, are also dense like embroidery stitch. So, the plaintiff should be pronounced guilty. As for the defendant, whether he is a cobbler, or steals, makes the mummy, as long as he rang the bell, he was not wrong, and the defendant's debate is very convincing, now he was sentenced to three full cups of yogurt, which should form the block, as bright as pearl, piece by piece, and the defendant need pay them off under the weather in May like half of August. However, the defendant also provides fodder and cotton, in order to block things in the throat. Both sides in the dispute must be reconciled, without payment of any fees. Sentencing is over!

[The others were dumbfounded, but responded with warm applause, chanting: "Master is wise, the law is supreme! Master is wise, the law is supreme!" The lights turn dark, and the following lights hit Bakhtin couple in the corner of the stage.]

Yelina: It is too ridiculous. The law is actually so mocked.

Bakhtin: Honey, sometimes a mess of confusion can be created in the name of the law!

Yelina: Rabelais's laughter has a powerful subversive force.

Bakhtin: Yes, honey, this is an interesting and serious subject that I was thinking and researching. The truth can be told with a smile.

Yelina: But in the face of this situation now, how can we laugh out?

"End"

3

"Act Ⅳ "

(In 1952, on the scene of Doctoral Dissertation Defense, there was one chairman of the committee, four professors and two scorers, as well as several observers, including Bakhtin's wife Yelina. The answerer on a pair of crutches was Bakhtin. The staff shouted:"Please professors and students have a seat, the dissertation defense keeps going!" Everyone has a seat, and put down the coffee cup and cup in the hands at random.)

Chairman: Well, professors and classmates, Mr. Bakhtin just spent two hours giving concise and comprehensive explanation and statement on research methods, historical background and the main points of his dissertation "Rabelais theory" made highlights. Now the professors of the defense committee can raise questions, and then Mr. Bakhtin answers.

Professor A: First of all, please allow me to pay tribute to Mr. Bakhtin. Mr. Bakhtin, you are 57 years old this year, and your age is still older than mine. Six years ago, your paper was submitted to the Academic Degrees Committee to review in public, but failed to pass. After that, you carried out modifications and additions carefully according to the experts' advice. We all know that your health is not optimistic, while academic research is hard work. Oh, I particularly ...... I mean, the perseverance of your spirit, attitude and willpower make me admire indeed, at the same time, make me feel confused, I ...... I ......do you understand what I mean?

Bakhtin: Mr. Professor, no, I should call you Professor comrade, which is more in line with the times. I seem to understand what you mean. My wife (turn round and point Yelina) often raises some questions as similar as you. Yes, I'm almost six years old, and get sick, with a popular saying of China to describe my state at this time, I am "almost buried to the neck by the loess", the coffin and grave are very close to me. PhD for me is just a funeral wreath, dispensable. To be honest, Moscow or St. Petersburg city registration is more important than the degree certificates, it can help me more easily to see a doctor at least, and can make us enjoy more a little non-staple food supplied for residents in the capital. However, the question involved in this paper is equally important. Among all the great writers of world literature, Rabelais is very unfamous in our country, needed to be researched most, and the understanding and evaluation for him is also the most inadequate. Belinsky said that Rabelais was a great genius, is Voltaire in 16th century. In many scholars' view, in terms of the strength of his art and thought, as well as his historical significance, Rabelais should be comparable to Shakespeare, Cervantes. Rabelais was important in deciding the fate of the French literature, and played a key role in deciding the fate of the world literature. People get the humor of the folk culture from Rabelais's novel, namely, laugh at thousands of years of cultural development. He expressed the folk laughter best in the field of literature. So, before I dragged my sick body to creep to the tomb of death, I am accompanied by Rabelais' ancient, hearty and happy laughter and happy, and I[3] feel on top of the world in my heart!

Illustrator: Gustave Dore

Professor A: Thank you, Mr. Bakhtin, I rise to pay tribute to you!

Professor B: Mr. Bakhtin, your paper has the informative

historical materials, well-argued, logical, glistened with wisdom and thought, and I was inspired after reading, and benefited. My question is why you wanted to select the "laugh", such a relatively small and light matter, to write such a masterpiece?

Bakhtin: Thank you for your question. Just as what you said, the word "laugh" is inconspicuous, and just as the folk's joke to make a smile never contends against the slogan of the great politics. Laughter belongs to the folk, the public, and nobody. It looks humble, small, vulgar, but it is the master key to unlock the mystery of mankind! In a certain sense, the history of mankind is the history of jokes. Human beings were suffering in laughter, and pursue happiness in misery. Sometimes, laughter is that we can only carry a weapon for self-defense and entertainment. Laughter can keep us away from fear and pain. Laughter is also a force to correct and amend, and it can prevent human from fast alienation at a fast speed.

Professor C: I'm sorry, Mr. Bakhtin, please allow me to interrupt you. I have been thinking a problem for a long time, and it has been lingering in my mind. I wanted to ask you for advice early, so I can not wait to want to raise questions to you, please forgive me!

Bakhtin: You're welcome. Please!

Professor C: My question is, my question is ...... (anxiously scratching and racking his head) Damn, I am so sorry, I thought this issue for many years, but I can not remember it suddenly. The problem is ...... The problem is ...... my head is really disappointing, it's a shame, where is my problem at the moment? It's clearly in sight.

Chairman: Professor Sholokhov, please sit down, do not scratch and rack your head. Keep calm. Temporarily forgetting things is a common disease, I have an aunt, this disease often happens to her, who is always looking for the key while she is going to open the door, and she often forgets to hold her dog when walking the dog in the morning, and after walking in the cold for two hours, she did not find that her dog was still in the house until going home.

Professor C: What you said can not be trusted, because I know, actually you do not have any aunts, and I am not Sholokhov as well.

Chairman: Look, my memory is not as good as you do! Haha, are there professors to raise question?

Professor D: Mr. Bakhtin, it can be seen from your articles that "laughter" is the core concept of your carnival theory. You think carnival laughter has a profound and complex nature. Can you can use a few brief words to summarize the complex and profound nature?

Bakhtin: Okay. Carnival laughter is a unique humor of the festival. It is not the individual response to a single and ridiculous phenomenon. First of all, carnival laughter is universal, and everyone can laugh. Secondly, it is all-encompassing, it involves all things and people. The whole world looks ridiculous, you can feel and understand it from the point of laughter. Finally, this laughter has a dual nature. It is not only happy and exciting, but also cynical, negative and positive, burial and regeneration.

Professor C: (suddenly rise, laughing) I think of it, my question, I think of it. What did you say just now? Hurry up, remind me! Oh, I know, I know, it is "The whole world looks ridiculous", do you say it like this, right?

Bakhtin: Yes.

Professor C: Do you think I am ridiculous?

Bakhtin: You might be an exception.

Professor C: I am firmly opposed to laughing. In my humble opinion, laughter makes me feel very uncomfortable. There is nothing so funny. Everything in the world is ridiculous? This view is very unserious, very dangerous. Our government is ridiculous? Our beloved Comrade Stalin is ridiculous?

Bakhtin: Professor comrade, please not be too excited. The object I studied is the medieval folk culture five hundred years ago, which is entirely expanded on the base of Rabelais' "Giant". Seriousness is official, imperious, combined with violence, prohibitions, restrictions. In this seriousness, there is always the part of fear and intimidation. Your question just makes me feel it. On the contrary, laughter and humor have to overcome fear as a precondition. Power and authority will never use the language of humor to speak. Laughter and humor is always the weapon of freedom in the masses' hands. I repeat: the medieval laughter and humor is definitely the unofficial, but it is legal. Of course, the freedom of the folk's laugh, like any kind of freedom, is just relative, but never eradicated in history.

Professor C: Mr. Bakhtin, why do you think the seriousness is wrong?

Bakhtin: I have already said, it is in contrast to humor, I mean, it is in contrast to the culture of laughter, the medieval solemnity is internally full of fear, weakness, obedience, lies, hypocrisy, resulting in intimidation, threats and prohibitions. Solemnity threatens human beings, makes demands, and enacts the prohibitions by the power; for the subordinate, solemnity treads on eggs, gentle and submissive, sycophant, applauds. Thus, the seriousness caused the people's distrust. This is in a bureaucratic tone, like all the official things, always posturing. Seriousness is oppressive, frightening, and restrained. It openly lies, hypocritical and false. On the feast, and on the table, as well as in Festival Place, the serious tone as the mask was abandoned, in humorous, funny, parodic, ironic and ridiculous situation, another truth began to spread! At that moment of joy, all the fear, worry and lies will vanish!

Chairman:(look at his watch) Good! Because of the time, today's thesis defense is over! Please wait a moment, I'll announce the result.

(Chairman and another four members whisper to each other)
Illustrator: Ma Wenzhe
Chairman: I am sorry, keep you waiting! (He clears his throat, according to the transcript that has been drafted in advance, solemnly reads off it) The doctoral dissertation "Rabelais theory " Mr. Bakhtin's submitted has constantly had the supplement of new results by six years of repeatedly modification, its quality was greatly improved. The topic selection of the thesis is novel, and the method is right, with a lot of historical materials, and plenty of argumentation and distinctive viewpoint. It fills in a gap which should not happen to the Soviet academic world in the study of the western literature. The work will become a classic in all likelihood and be passed down in history. In view of this, the doctoral thesis defense committee agreed that, after careful study, this work has fully reached a doctoral

dissertation level, now we decide to confer on Mr. Bakhtin the title of Master's Degree. It is over, please everyone applaud him!

Bakhtin: I protest, do you make a mistake? I applied for a PhD!

Chairman: Mr Bakhtin, please calm down, do not so serious! Like you, an old man and have so much knowledge. Who cares what your degree?

Bakhtin: They both are irrelevant things totally!

Chairman: how are they irrelevant? You know, the world has widespread contact. A sneeze in Moscow could lead to an upheaval in Hungary absolutely.

Bakhtin: But it has anything to do with my thesis?

Chairman: Mr. Bakhtin, it does not matter seemingly, in fact, there is a strong relationship between them, simply causality. You think, if what you studied was not Rabelais, but Stalin and Gorky, or any Soviet writer, and the results may be completely different. Do you understand what I mean?

Bakhtin: I do not understand, and completely confused!

Chairman: The Chinese people have a wisecrack, "you have understood, but pretend not to know". You should not be such a person, right? You still think about it carefully!

Yelina: Honey, you accept the result! As what you said, everything in the world is ridiculous.

The others: Yes, yes, Mr. Bakhtin, everything is ridiculous.

(Everyone clapped his hands, jumped up and down, upbeat music started.)

"End"

"Act V "

(Contemporary era. In the university classroom, a professor
is working with a dozen students in the classroom discussion,
and everyone is sitting around together, the atmosphere is
relaxed, casual. The professor is standing in the middle.)
Professor: how about it, everyone? About Bakhtin's carnival
theory, I've taught systematically, in this classroom
discussion, you can freely express your opinions, we share
your feelings and experiences.
A girl: Professor, does this seminar have scores? I mean, you
give us scores.
B boy: Girl, you too care about it, you say without any loss.
A girl: If what I will say is nothing, I have the right to
remain silent and I do not want to waste my spittle.
Professor: Everyone must speak, and today's discussion will
serve as a reference for final exam of this course.
A boy: I am first to open the subject for discussion! Anyway,
everyone has to speak, or we can't pass the exam. I start first,
please everyone neglect my unwisdom.
B boy: Hurry up, if you have something or songs to say. Whatever
you have, please hurry up. You do not spend a long time on
the prelude. We are from the northeast, and we are flustered
as soon as feeling anxious.
A girl: Calm down, calm! Let him finish it!
A boy: Professor, I feel that Mr. Bakhtin's study is really
profound, ordinary people's brains can't be compared to his.
We usually have a joke, make fun, but we never feel "laugh"
has so many characteristics. After listening to your class,
and read his book, I come to think of it, maybe what he said

seemed to be very reasonable. Such as a few of words he said, I have copied them in a notebook, to keep them as the wisdom in mind for a lifetime. There are a few of what he said,

specially helpful, (reading according to the note) you hear: carnival laughter keeps people away from the oppression of those gloomy, such as the "eternal" "absolute" " adhere consistently" "unshakable". They are now facing the laugh of the happiness and freedom of the world, together with their unfinished and open nature......

C boy: Come on, stop, please! What wisdom is it? Prolixity, abstract and boring, not only obscure, but also obscure.

B girl: Exactly, the motto should be brief and agile. For example, laughter is the best gift God gave mankind. Man's laughter is God's consolation.

D boy: Oh, shit! Don't put God on your mouth. Do you think you are an angel? God will laugh when man thinks, and you can't let God happily roll on the floor.

B girl: Laughter is the only expression God doesn't have, have you seen God laugh?

D boy: No, I do not hurry to see him. But the reason that God does not laugh is because you think too little.

B girl: Go to hell. Everybody goes on to say mottoes.

B boy: Laughter is a corrective force that can prevent us from becoming weirdo.

A girl: Only human beings suffer in this world, so they had to invent "laugh"[3].

D boy: A life without loud talking and laughing is a lamp without oil! It's your turn! (Touch B girl)

B girl: the one who doesn't know how to laugh is usually an

arrogant and conceited guy.

E boy: If you laugh, then all the world will laugh with you. If you want to make snore, only you will wash and sleep alone!

A girl: A smile is the shortest distance between two people.

C boy: The girl's smile makes the world disorder.

B girl: So I do not laugh easily!

B boy: You really have a good sense of humor.

C girl: Humor is a seriousness hidden after the joke.

B boy: seriousness is to pretend! For what? Anyway, everybody on the earth knows that.

A girl: Humor is the most beautiful costumes people have in social situations.

A boy: it is the most high-end cosmetics!

B girl: Actually, humor is the buoy in the waves of life, one of tools to survive.

B boy: Ridicule is the euphemism for anger!

C girl: No! Ridicule is narrow-minded people's anger.

C boy: ridicule is a gentle test for the truth. You can laugh at everything, but that does not make the universe into a cartoon.

D girl: Haha, this sentence is powerful, grade.

D boy: A fool follows other people to laugh! If laughing too much, he will show his stupidity!

A girl: The fool's laughter is the loudest! Or, a loud laughter often shows his emptiness.

A boy: Who did say that?

A girl: Japanese.

A boy: what the Japanese said is the people's language, it doesn't count!

A girl: Laughter is spices of talking, not as a staple food.

You are not serious!

B boy: Earnest produces the comedy, and joke is a product from earnest.

Professor: So what about earnest?

B boy: Seriousness pretends to be earnest, or seriousness is not equal to earnest.

B girl: I agree with him. When we rationally treat the world, we will certainly laugh, if emotionally treating, we would surely cry.

C boy: the true source of humor and laughter is not the joy, but sorrow!

C girl: If you want to pursue a clear head, the only recipe is to laugh, and laughing can get rid of everything!

D boy: I respect and admire people who have a sense of humor, because if you can laugh, it means that you are in control of the situation. If the situation is bad, but you are able to find the humor in it, it means you are not intimidated by this bad situation.

D girl: But where to find such a rare animal?

A boy: Go to the theater, to see Benshan Zhao play sketches, or listen to Guo Degang' cross talk!

A girl:(pretend to vomit) I want to vomit! Disgusting!

B boy: Stephen Chow is okay?

A girl: He is too old, and we simply go back to the Neolithic Age together!

C boy: laughter is able to across the ages, I smile to die as soon as putting up Rabelais' novel, so have to put it down. Someday I will read it.

C girl: There were many writers like Rabelais, Cervantes in the history of Western literature. Their works are humorous.

I also read Gogol, Chekhov, Hasek, Richard Leacok's novels,
profound and interesting. But the Chinese writers always keep
a straight face!

D boy: You're not entirely correct. "Journey to the West" is
very funny! Mr. Mo Yan's novel, which just won the Nobel Prize
for Literature, is also quite exaggerated.

D girl: I don't like to read it!

D boy: That's because you've lost the ability to laugh, or
you are too stupid, what I said is just a possibility.

D girl: But I can't be still beyond you! You have fool genes!

Professor: Well, well, we just discuss the issue. You can't
be engaged in personal attacks! Well, you mentioned the loss
of ability to laugh, "Yuan Fang, how do you think?" (Point
to A boy)

A boy: Nope! We seem to have been laughing!

A girl: Idiot, you are to giggle. The professor refers to
Bakhtin-style laughter, with thinking and criticalness! Isn't
it, professor?

Professor: Maybe!

B boy: We're not in the Middle Ages. China doesn't have the
tradition of carnival.

Professor: If I allow you to organize a carnival by yourselves,
would you like to do it?

C boy: I am afraid not. Is it approved by the department and
the school?

B girl: Certainly it does not work, if gathering in the plaza
and playground, we have to report it to higher authorities
for approval.

D boy: If the principal, dean, department head were dressed
as a clown, and let students banter, ridicule, mock them and

even kick their asses arbitrarily, that will be disordered, we prepare to be expelled!

D girl: Professor, you can't play tricks on us, even if not expelled, we have to be punished such as a serious warning or probation. If we can't find work in future, how will we survive?

C boy: Even we dare not laugh at the chef in the canteen. The meals have been so bad, if we mock him, who can guarantee that he doesn't put flies, cockroaches into food, plus a spit!

Professor: Speaking of the canteen, I suddenly feel hungry. Oh, it is really time to eat. How about we can't be engaged in Carnival, but we can be engaged in a very small game? In a while, I am going to eat in the canteen with you, my treat!

Everyone: (clapping) Well, well, this game is good!

Professor: You really have promise, only want to eat! I mean, when we finish the meal, everyone will stain something such as a few rice grains, vegetable leaves or rice residue on your mouth, nose, cheeks or forehead deliberately, and then we come out together and see others how to respond, how about it, is it interesting, right?

Everyone: (shook their heads together) No!

Professor: Why? I feel it is very interesting, the students meeting with us on the way must be particularly strange, and look at us strangely, then they would roar with laughter.

A boy: Maybe they would call the police, and think that all our spirit goes wrong.

A girl: The staff in the canteen would prevent us out of the canteen. We are suspected to "package", with rice and leaves stained on our faces, and regarded as thief's behavior, we would be banned.

B boy: Exactly, if I am seen by my girlfriend incautiously, she would surely say I lose her dignity, she would jump from the building to commit suicide.

B girl: My boyfriend is also very thin-skinned, he can't stand this kind of stimulation.

C boy: If there was a group of onlookers following us, then we would be in a serious trouble, and security guards would arrest us to ask questions.

C girl: Oh, we are too young! Professor, please keep calm, and keep clear, okay?

D boy: Impulse is the devil, professor, why would you take the risk?

D girl: Professor, we all care about you! We should live as usual, there is no need to play carnival games, if there is a good thing, you can laugh secretly!

A boy: I agree with you, if the leadership asks you to talk for this thing without end, can't you bother?

B girl: maybe the school will let you write the check!

B boy: Must be! The school will definitely demote you, pay cut.

C girl: Even if you are not for your own sake, but for your wife and kids, you have to think about it.

Professor: Well, classmates, thank for your enlightenment, I... I ... I...... (choking) what should I say?

A girl: Professor, you do not say anything, and only invite us to eat enough.[3] You do not cry, Bakhtin said: "Everything in the world is ridiculous Professor (Wipe the canthus with his hand, sobbing): Yes, everything in the world is ridiculous. Come on, I invite you to lunch!

Everyone (cheering): Yeah, yeah! (rhythmically shouting

together) eat, drink! Eat, drink! Xishasha, Xishasha, Xishasha, Xishasha, yeah, yeah!

Everybody clapped each other, hugged. Upbeat music sounded, and everybody spontaneously danced hip-hop, filled with carnival atmosphere

"End"

3

Svejk

Today, you can encounter a person wearing shabby clothing in Prague's street. He doesn't simply know what position he actually plays in the history of this great new era. He takes his own way humbly, not to bother others, and there are no news reporters to bother him, and invite him to make a speech. If you ask his surname, he will answer simply and humbly: "Svejk."

In fact, this gentle and humble man, wearing shabby clothing, is our old acquaintance, courageous Svejk. As early as the reign of Austria, his name had been well-known by all the people in Czech Republic, and to the era of the Republic, his popularity has remained ever.

---- Yaroslav • Hasek

3

Characters

Hasek: a veteran and writer (acted by the same actor as Svejk)

Svejk: a Lukasz Captain orderly, more than thirty years old.

Mrs. Miller: Svejk's maid.

Lukasz: the first advance even Captain of the Austrian army's ninety-first regiment.

Katz: the army's priest. Svejk served him as an orderly.

Doob: a high school teacher originally, and the lieutenant of the ninety-first regiment now.

Malek: a recorder of the history of the camp.

Barry Horowitz: "Bei Bei Man" pub owner

Mrs. Barry Horowitz: "Bei Bei Man" pub landlady.

Wonica: the ninety-first regiment's quartermaster

The Chairman of the Social Committee for Relief, the captain of the gendarmerie, military police (two people), doctors, telephone operates, cooks, ordinary soldiers and officers, about ten people, pub customers (several people), one girl.

"Act I"

(The 1921 Spring. Prague Municipal Government Social Committee for Relief. The veteran Hasek comes to seek a job. Here is the same layout and furnishings as the office. The chairman of the committee crosses his legs resting on the table, whistling, leisurely reading the newspaper.)

Hasek:(on crutches) Excuse me, you're the chairman?

Chairman:(turn over newspapers, happily laughing) it's so funny, the great world is full of wonders. There is fresh news every day in Prague. Look, the governor of the bank of the young wife and his driver actually eloped. The governor was so angry that he wanted to jump, saying that the driver was really so pitiful! (then continue to read the newspaper)

Hasek: Sir, (knock the floor with a cane) excuse me ......

Chairman:(laugh again) Haha, a good news, there are a number of fresh girls in"Kuai Kuai Le "......

Hasek :(improve his voice) Chairman......

Chairman:(throw the newspaper in his hands on the desk, and back to normal posture) What happened? Don't you see I'm busy?

Hasek: I'm sorry, Mr. Chairman! Excuse me, sir! I would like to seek some help from the Social Committee for Relief.

Chairman: Help? What's your name, and what's your work, age, origin?

Hasek: My name is Jaroslav • Hasek, call me Svejk. My nominal age is forty, and no permanent job, to fend for myself, usually sell dogs.

Chairman: Sell dogs? Sell what kind of dogs?

Hasek: All kinds of dogs. If you like, I can send one to you. I have all kinds of grades, and the variety is complete beyond your imagination. All kinds of mongrel, dirty, degrading and homeless dogs are usually purchased at low prices by me, then washed and brushed, and given a fake ID of noble descent, and then sold to the rich at high prices. These people are generally stupid. You buy one!

Chairman: Shut up, you dare to scold me a fool.

Hasek: No, no, no! You're not a fool. You are a benevolent leader with wisdom.

Chairman: Well, well, don't be a nag! So, you're a dog dealer?

Hasek: Thank Mr. Chairman for your compliment!

Chairman: This is not a compliment, but compassion. If you were a dog, it would be nice, because here we would have a special Pet Protection Association to help you. Unfortunately, you're a dog dealer. So, you can't enjoy the benefits of help. Ah, if you were thirty years younger, it would be also easy to handle, and you could be helped by the children's welfare. You have nominal age forty, which doesn't conform to the conditions. Oh, yes, I almost forgot, are you in prison, that is to say, had you been convicted or spent time in prison?

Hasek: I have been never sued.

Chairman: That's too bad! You don't comply with relief conditions of those who have been released for the labor camp. Let me think, by the way, you are always drinking, right?

Hasek: Not at all, I never drink.

Chairman: I'm sorry, alcoholic helping center can't help you. It appears that[3] you aren't a girl stumble into abyss of suffering, really no way! You should have stolen anything, right?

Hasek: I am not a thief. I have been a soldier, and participated in World War II.

Chairman: I don't really help! It's not useful. If you cracked a crib, even if you pick up something on the sly, you would have a place to go, have meals, but you weren't caught.

Hasek: No, I didn't do it simply.

Chairman: It's more difficult to deal. Take you to the riffraff shelter? But you look as if you were a man wearing clothing decently, otherwise, you would be able to receive a relief fund.

Hasek: I don't want any relief, I just want to find something to work. No matter what it is, even if it is very hard, I am not afraid yet.

Chairman: What? Are you kidding, man? Are you forcing to do what is beyond my ability? Even I have nothing to do here, and idle all day, you still join in. God, how unlucky I am today that meeting you! Come on. I am going to see the drama " Svejk " soon. Don't delay my business, please!

Hasek: I am just Svejk.

Chairman: What? You are Svejk? Are you kidding me? He is a clown and hero in Czechs' mind, you dare to impersonate yet?

Hasek: I didn't lie. I am Svejk who people talk about everywhere, a real idiot identified by the official agency.

Chairman: Haha, look carefully, you really look like him! What are you laughing? How impolite you are! Stand at attention! Serious! Turn back! After I count three numbers you immediately disappear from my eyes! One, two, three! (Svejk left) Look, this guy on the crutches runs so fast. Ha ha ha, he thought he was Svejk, don't take me for a fool! Oh, " Svejk" opens at once! The chairman left in a hurry.

"End"

"Act Ⅱ"

(A shabby living room. A chair, Svejk reclined on a chair, is concentrating on reading the newspaper. A round table, on which a few cups of coffee maker were placed. Mrs. Miller, the old nanny, is making coffee.)

Svejk: Mrs Miller, please come here.

Mrs. Miller:(come his chair) What's up, sir?

Svejk:(give a sign, ask her to sit on a chair beside him, who looks solemn) I want to enlist, join the army to serve the country, go to the front to fight!

Mrs. Miller:(put her hand on Svejk's forehead) Sir, have you a fever? How are you raving in the daylight?

Svejk: I didn't fever, never so sober. The newspaper said, there is a dark cloud hanging over our dear motherland. The enemies attack our country from North and South, we are being beaten. It's okay if we are attacked from one direction, the key is to be attacked from both sides, it goes too far. It seems that I have to go into battle personally.

Mrs. Miller: But you are sick from head to toe, and can't move, lying in bed, still need me to take care of you, how can you fight?

Svejk: It's okay, nothing can stop a patriot to charge forward. In addition to two legs out of control, there is no problem in other parts of my body, absolutely to serve as cannon fodder. Mrs. Miller, you don't like reading newspapers at ordinary times, don't care about national affairs. Look, the heroic deeds on this newspaper are so moving! You read this message on the " Prague Official News ", about the volunteer Dr. Joseph • Waugh Young. Let me read it: He was stationed in Galicia seventh cavalry battalion. In the fierce combat, a bullet got into his head. When his comrades were going to carry him to bandage, he cried: it's a little wound, and there is no need to bandage. Hardly did the last word disappear, he rushed up again. But his legs were also broken by the grenade. People wanted to carry him away, but he pushed assistant nurse, jumping on one leg toward the line of fire, fended against the enemy with a walking stick. But a piece of shrapnel flew over, his hand on the crutch was blown up. He used the other hand to hold the crutch, shouted: " Rush, go ahead for victory " Finally, he was ripped apart. His head was still rolling off the ground quickly towards the enemy position, still shouting : "We should be bravely fighting the enemy! Long live the emperor!" You listen, Mrs. Miller, compared with these heroic soldiers, my disease is simply nothing.

Mrs. Miller: Newspapers is boasting all day, do you believe it either?

Svejk: Whether you believe it or not, anyway, I believe. Come on. Get to the street to buy me a service cap, and borrow a wheelchair from the old man of candy store. The crutches are off the rack, and I'll go to conscription committee to report.

 (Loudly sing "The sun rises in the east, we rushed to the battlefield, not afraid of bleeding, not afraid of becoming meat paste, rush! Rush!")

Mrs. Miller:(keep playing the apron with her hands, and circling back and forth in the same place) Oh, I shouldn't buy army uniform, but go to the doctor to give you a little sedative!

(Mrs. Miller leaves. Svejk is still loudly singing, "Bei Bei Man". The pub landlady Mrs. Barry Horowitz comes on.)

Mrs. Barry Horowitz: (sobbing) Svejk, help me, I couldn't live anymore.

Svejk: Oh, what happened, madame? "Bei Bei Man" pub is run at a loss? I haven't been there to drink beer for a week, and I'm greedy.

Mrs. Barry Horowitz: It's more serious than losing money! My husband was captured by policemen secretly without reasons, and sentence to ten years.

Svejk: Oh, no, without any crimes, would he be in jail for ten years? Honestly, I can't understand. Was there a little bit of reason when he was captured?

Mrs. Barry Horowitz: Really no. You know my husband. He is usually humble, afraid of snowflakes hitting his head, never talk about politics. A few days ago, the spy asking about guests' ideological trends in the pub all day chatted with my husband when nobody is there, but my husband hums and refused to say a word. The spy was very disappointed, and suddenly asked a sentence when left, saying that how the emperor's portrait previously hanging on the wall was gone. My husband said, because the portrait was covered with flies' feces, it was put away and placed in the attic. For this sentence, the spy made him in trouble, saying he committed the crime of blasphemy emperor, then my husband was taken away. Flies defecated on the emperor's portrait, so they should be caught, right?

Svejk: Damn flies, police won't forgive them! Caution is the source of all wisdom! Ten years are slightly long. In the past I have said, if committing little crime, you will be sentenced up to five years. Hey, think positively, Mrs. Barry Horowitz, don't cry, fortunately not to be sentenced to two years, or three years.

(Mrs. Miller took a doctor to come on the stage.)

Mrs. Miller: Sir, this is the doctor I invited, let him see your disease, and prescribe some sedative.

Doctor :(move towards the recliner) Mr. Svejk, would you please put your tongue out. Your servant Mrs. Miller said that you have a fever.

Svejk: Doctor, I have no disease. Please go back where you came. Don't listen to Mrs. Miller's nonsense. I have very good health, and tomorrow morning I am going to fight on the front lines, to serve their country.

Mrs. Miller: Sir, you let the doctor have a look, and take the pills, you will be sober, at least let the doctor have a look at your legs.

Svejk: Please the doctor get out quickly. I'm not sick, you are sick!

Doctor: It seems that you are really kinda sick, because the patients always consider they are not sick, just as the drunk people never admits that he was drunk. I can give you a proof, which maybe make you exempt from military service.

Svejk: Shut up, get out of here, I want to sing military song!

Doctor: You're a really good guy! For three months, in ten thousand young men through my examination, nine thousand nine hundred ninety-nine people were malingering to evade military service, only one stroke and died in front of me. I let them put this malingering corpses carried away.

Svejk: Doctor, you are so smart. How did you conduct the medical examination?

Doctor: It's very simple. For those who claimed themselves to have TB, rheumatism, cancer, swollen hernia, gastritis, typhoid, diabetes, pneumonia, etc., I took the following measures: (1) a strict diet, drink a glass of ice water in morning and evening for three days; (2) all people took large doses of quinine laxative; (3) gastric lavage with one liter of warm water twice a day; (4) clysis with soapy water and glycerin enema; (5) wrap with a sheet soaked by ice water when sleeping. Generally adhering to the enema stage, those who pretended to be sick said that they had been better, begging, their only desire was to immediately follow the advance battalion to go to the battlefield. Only a handful of people can survive after five stages, eventually being put into simple coffin and sent to the cemetery and buried.

Mrs. Miller: We don't trouble you, doctor. Anyway, he said he was not sick, and tomorrow go to the front line directly.

Doctor: No, I still give him a check here! Of course, I won't take the means I said just now. I just ask a few simple questions, please Mr. Svejk answer me truthfully. First, do you know how long the circumference of the earth is?

Svejk: I don't know. I didn't measure it, and I couldn't find such a long ruler.

Doctor: Well, then, do you believe Armageddon?

Svejk: I have to see the doomsday.

Doctor: Third, can you calculate how much the deepest place of Pacifice is?

Svejk: Please forgive me, I can't. But, I would also like to ask the doctor for solving a mystery: There is a building with three floors, with eight windows on each floor, and two chimneys on the roof, and four tenants to live each floor, now you tell me which year this building janitor Grandma died?

Doctor: I think, (keep silent for a while) I can't give an

answer. But I still want to ask you for a math problem, what is 12864 multiplied by 38765.

Svejk: Two hundred and fifty!

Doctor: OK, I write a medical certificate to you! If necessary, you can take it out to make a proof when necessary.

Svejk: Thank you!

Doctor: Good luck, you are a good guy, see you!

Svejk: I hope so! I really worry about your health.

(Doctor leaves, and Mrs. Miller see him off.)

Svejk: This a stupid doctor, looking very bad, with a short-lived appearance of ghosts, who dares to promise him to "see you".

(Mrs. Miller turns back to go)

Svejk: Mrs. Miller, are you ready for the cap and wheelchair?

Mrs. Miller: Yes, sir.

Svejk: Fetch the cap. I won't wait tomorrow. You use a wheelchair to carry me to leave now, and go to join the army!

 (Mrs. Miller pushes out the wheelchair, helps Svejk to sit, and put the crutches on Svejk's legs horizontally, pushes him to go round the scene, slowly walk down.)

Svejk: (waving crutches, and shouting all the way) to join the army is glorious, loyal to the emperor, go to hit Belgrade! Destroy the enemy! Go to hit Belgrade! Destroy the enemy!

 "End"

3

"Act Ⅲ"

(Lukasz Captain's living room. A rectangular dining table is covered with a plaid tablecloth, and a few chairs are placed around it. Four people sitting at the table are playing cards, and three people standing at the table are watching.)

Lukasz: Haha, I win again. Pay for it, you, and you, fast to pay for it, a hundred kroner per person, and a penny can't be owed.

Officer A: It's so bad today! I've lost three innings successively.

Officer B: I'm also so unlucky, alas, unlucky in love, and unlucky in the casino. Yesterday, my bitch actually made love with the orderly I just hired, and I caught them in the blanket. He also dared to touch with prefectorial lover, really so audacious. I ordered the men to tie him to a tree, and put the dog to bite his lower body, fuck vent my hate!

Lukasz: Dude, the orderly I now employ is a nuisance. Who always signs in despair all day, always writes home, and steals anything that he sees. Even if he is hit, it doesn't work, either. I knock his head as soon as I see him, but he doesn't remember the lesson. I've knocked out half of his teeth, but this guy doesn't obey yet. I really have no ideas! Fortunately, he doesn't dare make love with my woman.

(Lukasz is shuffling while chatting, and others are drinking beer, and laughing. The Katz father is drunk and comes on the stage,[3] and Svejk supports Father with his hands.)

Katz Father: Dear Lukasz Captain, my little baby, and my dear, officers friends, aha, I have been missing you on behalf of Christ and his wife.

Lukasz: It seems Katz father has been drunk again. When did Christ have a wife?

Katz Father: I told you, one respects the father, and the one respects Christ; one despises the father, and the one despises Christ, because the Father is the incarnation and representative of God and Christ. So, I spend my time with prostitutes in the brothel, drink, which also experiences the beauty of a woman for the body of Christ. Haha, my dear comrades, I forgot to introduce you to my new orderly. Come on, you see, he is called Svejk, who is the most lovable idiot I've ever seen, a rare clown.

Svejk: Father, you're so flattering! Respected officers, my name is Svejk, meeting with you is my good fortune on the base of past life, and thank you for your ancestors.

Katz Father: Gentlemen, you certainly don't know where he came from. This fool is picked up by me. Do you know where? Not from the garbage, but from a lunatic asylum. That's too funny! He is simply a gift from God for Christmas. I have promised to betroth my sister to Svejk, but you know that in fact I don't have a sister.

Svejk: Father is very generous, drunk each time, always ordered me to slap him in the face, and declared his value was equivalent to a pig's, ordered that I can't underestimate him.

Lukasz: Oh, my God, how can you stay in a lunatic asylum?

Svejk: I don't understand either, sir. I was originally going to join the army, my old maid Mrs. Miller pushed me with a wheelchair, and I shouted "Long live the emperor, bravely fight the enemy, victory belongs to us" all the way, drawing many onlookers. Later he was taken to the madhouse.

Officer A: He was just put into the madhouse!

Svejk: An officer also said that like you. He said "I fully appreciate your patriotism, but the way of performance and the occasion are not proper. He also said, your patriotic performance might or would be even inevitably seen as a mockery by the public, rather than the serious and solemn sincerity.

Lukasz: You've suffered in a lunatic asylum, right? That is not a good place to live.

Svejk: Over the left, sir. That is the best place I've ever been to.

Lukasz: Bullshit, you're an idiot.

Svejk: What I said is the truth, sir. I really don't understand why those madmen who put into the asylums are angry. There you can wear nothing on the floor to roll, learn to howl, bark, and even can bite. But, if you do that in the street, anybody seeing that will make a fuss. This is commonplace there, which is not surprising. In the madhouse, there is a kind of freedom that socialists couldn't even dream of, even though some people are tied to a pillar all day. You can see yourselves as God or the Virgin Mary, as the King of England or France queen. There was an old man shouting that he was the archbishop, who didn't do anything else, only gobbled to eat, and brazenly defecated. There was a man who insisted that he was a pregnant woman, to invite each of us to go to his infant baptism. There were still many poets, politicians, Boy Scouts, philatelists and amateur photographer. I met several professors, among them, an old professor was always chasing me to explain that the birthplace of gypsy was Beijing Haidian of China, Another professor was endlessly to show me that there was a sphere as a hundred times as itself in the earth inside.

Lukasz: Shut up, stupid, the tongue was running in your mouth, that's nonsense. If I were Katz father, I would break your ribs one by one.

Svejk: Katz father also said so. He is a kind man, and expressed, broke two once. However, he falls asleep now, every time he first played mad after drunk, and then snored like this.

Lukasz: Shut up, you're a glib bum. If you are caught by me one day, I will let you suffer from my iron fist. (He moves to Svejk, and put his fist under his nose.)

Svejk: Yes, sir. I have smelled out the grave.

Lukasz: Hum, you should continue to be put you into the lunatic asylum.

Svejk: Thank you very much! I really like that place, where I was just as happy as in heaven! I can say anything casually, don't worry about other people to snitch. You can shout, yell, cry, laugh; you can crawl away, and run backwards; you can also hop on one leg. It's the happiest days of my life I spent in the lunatic asylum.

Lukasz: Wake up Katz father, and ask him to discipline this beast who doesn't know the rules!

Svejk: I think it's better in the madhouse. I met you as soon as coming out, and always ordered me to shut up. If you don't believe, you can go to the lunatic asylum to live for days. You will certainly adapt there.

Lukasz :(Shake vigorously Katz father sitting on a chair and napping) Wake up, [3]wake up! If you don't discipline your orderly, I'll immediately shoot him!

Svejk: It doesn't work, he won't wake up. I can do it!

(Svejk moves to Katz priest, "PaPa", hits him in the face twice.)

Katz Father: Oh, oh, oh, drink, drink, drink!

Lukasz: Oh, oh, oh, what fuck you cry?! You look like a tomcat caterwauling! What fuck you drink?! As a father following the army, you're the raiser of soldiers' souls. Look at your actions, simply as a fucking shit!

Katz Father: Lukasz Captain, are you praising me? I tell you, as long as the country still believes that God has to bless them before soldiers die on the battlefield, in that way, father's office is a fat job to make money. I don't carry ammunition, and don't need to brave gunfire. In the past, I have to follow the officer's order to act, but now I can do whatever I want. I represent a character virtually nonexistent, and play the God's role. Do you think who you are, dare to lecture me? If I don't want to forgive your sins, it will be useless even if you are to kneel to me!

Svejk: Lukasz Captain, please don't take offense! This is what he is like you seeing him. If you both abuse each other, you can't win, I dare to bet with you! When sermoning on the pulpit, he can speak for hours, without drinking. If dirty and obscene words he used are compiled into a book, then it must be thicker than Encyclopedia. Really, you continue to play cards! Don't waste good time for who is shit.

Katz Father: right, play cards, Svejk is right! Come on, I also join in.

(Touch pockets, turn over all the pockets) where is my money, how do I have no[3] penny? Svejk, lend me two hundred crowns.

Svejk: Father, thank you for thinking highly of me. But if I had two hundred, I would go to open the bank.

Katz Father: Lend all the money you have to me, you should have twenty kroner?

Svejk: Father, originally I had indeed twenty kroner, but last night you borrow them to pay for a hooker in the brothel!

Katz Father: Fuck, you're an idiot and ass. You really lost my face! Hey, Lukasz captain, how about lending me one hundred kroner? I'll return you after I win!

Lukasz: How do you know that? If you lose, how do you return?

Katz Father: Mr. Captain, you look down on me extremely? Well, I use my orderly Svejk as collateral. If I lose, he will belong to you!

Lukasz: Except him, there is nothing else?

Katz Father: There is a "Bible", which can be mortgaged to you.

Lukasz: You still use this fool as the bet, one hundred crowns, anyway, I am going to find a new one instead of the old! Come on, let's start!

Katz Father: Come on, I bet one hundred crowns.

Lukasz: Me too.

Officer A: 100.

Officer B: Absolutely 100.

(Licensing.)

Lukasz: Haha, I win.

Katz father :(use his hands to hold his head) My God, where do you go at the key moment? My bad luck. My fortune is too bad. I had an "Ace", as a result, I got a "ten". The banker had a "Jack" firstly, but finally he also got the "Blackjack". I have no idea. It's bad luck. Svejk, I'm sorry, you were thrown to the devil Lukasz captain once.

Svejk: It's okay, father, anyway, you lost sooner or later, but it's so fast, I'm surprised as well. Don't be sad, I'm not on your side to serve you, but you're the friend with God, who won't treat you unfairly.

Katz Father: I'm sorry, we have to break up! Svejk, nobody can be against fate!

Svejk: You're right, father, you have to think positively as well. (Turn round, and salute to Lukasz captain) Excuse me, sir, I was Svejk just thrown to you by Katz father. Now report officially to you, obey your orders, obey your commands, over, please indicate!

Lukasz: Katz father recommend you to me, I hope you won't lose his face.

Svejk: Don't worry, Mr. Captain. Katz father's face was lost twenty years ago.

Lukasz: Don't interrupt, not allowed to interrupt the officer's speech! Let me speak frankly. There have been a dozen orderlies serving me, but no one can do for a long time. I am always strict with my soldiers, in this respect, I am well known. Only you make a bit of minor mistakes, then you will be severely punished. You must perform all my commands without complaint. I let you jump into the fire pit, you have to jump! Where do you see?

Svejk: (looking around) I'm looking for the fire pit!

Lukasz : (gnashing) Svejk, in the world there are always some wiseacre who is a fool in the others' eyes, do you understand these words?

Svejk: Yes, sir, just between you and me.

Lukasz: Cut the cackle, go to pack the luggage. We are going to the front line soon. Damn, the command to set out has been issued three times, but we aren't allowed to take action! (The officer stands up and leaves.)

Svejk: Sir, don't set out urgently, the first two batches

setting out have been taken as prisoners, and even the captain
did not come back.

Lukasz: Shut up, you're the most stupid person in the world,
Get out!

"End"

"**Act** IV"

(The office of gendarme detachment in Pu Jin Mu village. Two military policemen are reprimanded by the captain.)

Captain: Keep standing well, follow my password: Dress right, left dress, turn round!

Gendarme A: Captain, where to turn in the end?

Gendarme B: Captain, you should think carefully, and then speak. You have not accurate ideas extremely!

Captain: Shut up, idiots, drunks, and beasts! Only drink every day, always delay my work. (Point to the gendarme A) You! Where to look? I refer to you! Let you find a few fellows to go to the village to investigate residents' state of mind and degree of loyalty to the emperor, how about it?

Gendarme A: I went, sir, but no one was willing to become such a villainous spy, and refused to denounce their neighbors and friends.

Captain: You're foolish, didn't you say we pay them a bonus?

Gendarme A: They didn't do it even if given money.

Captain: (turn his head towards the gendarme B) What are you fuck laughing? Stand up straight, bullock! Still laughing? You'll cry! Let you catch deserters, how many?

Gendarme B: None, sir.

Captain: Deadbeat, idiot, ass! You have eyes to breathe? Can you not notice a suspicious man?

Gendarme B: Yes![3]

Captain: What? Where? You let him free?

Gendarme B: Too many deserters, fully more than a hundred people, who went towards the south together. I could catch all of them, and be rewarded for a meritorious action, but

I tried my best to persuade everyone, finally they let me go.

Captain: Coward, I'm going to send you to the military tribunal! (Captain is restlessly pacing to and fro in the room, suddenly pick up all kinds of files piled up a bunch on the table to throw in the air, and his hands scratch his head, growling.) You're idiots, can't you think for me?! Look, these are all kinds of notices, bulletins, questionnaires, instructions and commands from the higher authorities, too numerous to enumerate. The data are needed today and the material will be needed tomorrow; they are going to train spies, and will pay attention to deserters, spies, but there are only three men in our village gendarme detachments. No, you're not, at most, should be pigs. This job can't continue!

Gendarme A: Sir, those materials and files are used to deceive others, you don't pay attention to them, just fill up the numbers and then report them to the higher authorities. The other villages are also to do like this, anyway, they don't see them.

Gendarme B: Yeah, yeah! Captain, you feel relieved, I get two bottles of the finest rums again, We are going to have a good drink tonight!

Captain: Shut up, two sycophants, what are you fuck doing here? Get out of here, go to patrol, to catch deserters and spies! (Two gendarmes leave, and Svejk comes on, humming all the way, and excitedly going round the stadium.)

Svejk: It's also hice not to catch the train. Walking all the way can make me enjoy countryside views. It's just over five hundred miles away from the station. It's too close. If a little further away, it would be better.

Gendarme B: Stop! What are you doing?

Svejk: Hi, man, you don't recognize, I'm a soldier.

Gendarme A: Soldier? Not to go to the front line, but walk here, do what?

Svejk: I'm going to the front!

Gendarme B: Walk to the front line? Hehe, you can really play a joke. The front line is in the opposite direction!

Svejk: Really? I just asked an old woman for the direction. She pointed to this road! However, it doesn't matter, anyway, the earth is round, just I will walk longer.

Gendarme A: Hehe, your thinking is actually positive. Come on, follow us to find a place to rest and drink water!

Svejk: Well, thank you very much! I always met good friends along the way!

(Gendarmerie office.)

Captain: What's your name you just said?

Svejk: Excuse me, Svejk.

Captain: Where are you going?

Svejk: I'm going to my regiment, sir!

Captain: What place is your regiment?

Svejk: In Budejovice, sir.

Captain: But you obviously came from Budejovice! Budejovice has been already in your behind!

Svejk: Am I faint? (Suddenly raise his voice) Anyway, I'm just going to the ninety-one regiment in Budejovice!

Captain: Yelling is meaningless. Well, please sit down, welcome, Svejk! So you're probably on the wrong way, in fact, you're walking along the opposite direction of your destination, for this point, I can easily confirm to you. Here is a map of the Czech Republic, you have to have a good look at it.

Svejk:(Glance at the map) I don't understand this stuff, thickly dotted, like a cobweb. I feel dizzy! I have to listen to you.

Captain: Well! I ask you, where did you set out?

Svejk: Tabor.

Captain: What did you do at Tabor?

Svejk: Waiting for the train bound for Budejovice.

Captain: Why didn't you get on the train?

Svejk: Because I had no ticket.

Captain: Each soldier should receive a free ticket, they didn't give it to you!

Svejk: Yes, but I lost it in the car.

Captain: You were not on the train, how could you lose it in the car?

Svejk: I was through there from another place, and I didn't get off.

Captain: Didn't get off, how did you get here?

Svejk: how didn't you understand it yet? I was Lukasz Captain's orderly, as soon as the command of setting out to battle was launched, I carried his seven or eight boxes to squeeze into the carriage.

Captain: Seven or eight box? How many in the end, seven or eight?

Svejk: Both seven and eight. It was eight when I got on, and turn into seven when I got off. One was stolen by the thief.

Captain: Keep lying, no, keep going.

Svejk: Some people said I pulled the emergency brake on the train, then the train stopped. I saw there was a general without hairs on the train. He looked like a president of a bank very much, as a result, I annoyed him. To Tabor station, I got off to breath fresh air and drink a few glasses of wine, and the train left later. I was thrown like an orphan. The ticket and documents all were lost on the train, so I had to walk to catch up with my regiment.

Captain: Well, well, my head is so hurt that it seems to explode soon. Well, since you get to my place, you are my distinguished guest, for a while, let the cook do the dishes, I invite you to drink to recover from fatigue. You have a break first for a while, I go out, and right back.

(Captain moves to the corner of the stage, to make assignments to the other two gendarmes.)

Captain: keep your eyes widened, keep a close watch on him. You should become a little smarter, to learn from me. Look, I made him disoriented after a few questions.

Two gendarmes :(Unison) Captain is wise!

Captain: So, I'm the captain, you are absolutely not! We are going to urge him to drink tonight. The alcohol is the best polygraph, as long as he is drunk, even if he has a very strong will, his tongue will be out of control. He will obediently come clean on all the secrets, and then you can't stop him! Ha ha ha!

Two gendarmes :(in unison again) Captain is wise, captain is wise!

Captain: Get out! Go to prepare wine!

(the light dims, and all leave.)

(Lights grow brighter. On the next morning, three gendarmes are drunkenly lying on the ground. Svejk is making coffee aside.)

Captain :(wake up first, and call out) Ouch, ouch, killing me! My head seems to be kicked by a donkey, killing me! (Wake up suddenly) The Russian spy? He must run away! (He staggers to his feet, kicks the other two gendarmes) Get up, alcoholics! Get up, asshole! (Two gendarmes, "ouch, ouch", call out, struggling, but standing unstably!) Hurry….hurry…. hurry up, Svejk has gone!

(Voice hardly disappears, Svejk holds the coffee to come over.)

Svejk: Captain, two guys, come on, drink a cup of coffee to make the brain clear. You drank too much! Captain, please first, I'm going to cook a pot.

(Svejk leaves.)

Captain :(towards two gendarmes) It's really a shame, both of you are not beyond him even if being put together! Only a few glasses, you were as drunk as a fiddler! You still talked nonsense, and scolded your own government!

Gendarme A: Captain, you were drunk first, and still led us to shout: "Long live, Russia"

Gendarme B: I was sober at the beginning, but then heard the captain say that our emperor had been ill, and legs would be in the air soon! I was so scared that I was in a cold sweat!

Captain: Shut up, ungrateful bastard. You roared as a bull, lying on the ground and snoring firstly, how could you remember what I said?

Gendarme A: He's right! I can swear to God, you not only abused our emperor, but also said you would like to welcome the Russian tsar to serve as[3] the emperor of the Czech Republic!

Captain: Shit! If you dare talk nonsense, I'll put you in jail, then let your wife keep living alone all her life. You were drunk like a dead dog, but closed a pair of eyes as big as pig's. I've warned you, the alcohol is harmful, but neither of you close your ears. You lose your mind as soon as seeing wine. If he ran away, what should we do? How should we report to the leadership?

Gendarme A: But he hasn't, and look after us obediently! We were as drunk as a fiddler, and doors were open all night, if he wanted to escape, he could have a thousand chances. It seems that he is not a secret agent, spies. He was wronged!

Captain: You know what! This proves he is very sophisticated, with a strong will, calm. It would be nice if I have such a subordinate, so as to avoid being angry as soon as I see you!

Gendarme B: How should we treat him?

Captain: Let me carry on the interrogation of a few words to him. Hum, don't try to deceive me here under false pretenses!

(Svejk carries the coffee and comes on again.)

Svejk: Come on, come on, the coffee is very fragrant!

Captain: Yes. Svejk, can you take pictures?

Svejk: Yes!

Captain: Why don't you carry a camera?

Svejk: Because I don't have.

Captain: If you had a camera, then you must take pictures?

Svejk: Unfortunately, I haven't!

Captain: Is it difficult to take photos of the station?

Svejk: No, it's easier than I shoot people! Because the station doesn't move, keeps standing in a place, and no need to say: "Smile!"

Captain: I see! Well, Svejk, you tidy up later, I send someone to bring you to Pisek gendarmes' force, where it is easy for you to find your troops!

Svejk: Okay, thank you, captain, I'll go to wear a coat!

(Svejk leaves.)

Captain : (hurry up to sit at your desk and write a document, then look up and read it to the two gendarmes) "By my interrogation staggered, the prisoner has made a confession that he likes taking pictures, especially good at shooting the station. We haven' t found the camera on his body, but it's speculated that in order to escape the notice of others, he has hidden it in the other place, not carry it with him. The prisoner confessed that, if carrying the camera, he must take pictures, which is enough to prove that my speculation is not fictitious. " how about it, do you think how about this report presented to gendarmerie captain?

Two gendarmes : (Unison) The captain is the captain, captain is wise!

Captain: Well, you're in charge of escorting this guy to the gendarmerie brigade! Set out at once!

Gendarme A: Yes, ensure the completion of the task!

"End"

3

"Act V"

(In the train station waiting room as the temporary command post, four or five officers are discussing march plan and battle plan.)

(The long table is covered with a map, with a few cups. Lukasz is holding a magnifying glass and a pencil to stoop down to see the map. Doob lieutenant beside him holds a piece of telegram from the superior, pretentiously finds the next target with Lukasz captain together.)

Lukasz: What shit map, nowhere is right! In fact, here should have a mountain, but it can't be found on the map. There was originally a river, but it's the church marked on the map. According to the map, we should be in twenty meters underwater now.

Doob Lieutenant: Mr. Captain, you can't have a doubt about the map for military operation uniformly issued by the Department of Defense. It is our guide to march to war. Speaking of guides, who has brought a compass?

Lukasz: Quartermaster Wonika, come on, fetch a compass! Wonika, are you deaf? Hurry up, run, bring a compass!

Wonika: Excuse me, sir, I haven't the compass.

Lukasz: Fuck you! I just gave you the compass yesterday. You've lost it again?

Wonika: I'm sorry, it accidentally fell into the latrine when I went to the toilet last night.

Lukasz: You're lying, liar! You drank in exchange for it, right? I've actually known it!

Wonika:No, exchange a cigarette with a fellow.

Lukasz: Put him into the brig! I'll shoot you personally when my hands are free!

Doob Lieutenant: Alas! This is the result of usually lack of the ideological education. I have said, patriotism, devotion to duty, self-improvement, these are real weapons of soldiers in the war.

Lukasz: Doob Lieutenant, don't stand here to say words impractically. Come on, repeat the latest order of Brigadier.

Doob Lieutenant: Yes, sir! Brigadier simultaneously sent two orders. The one is to let us attack and occupy the western town Fort Gibson three days before; the other is to order we must march eastward.

Lukasz: Oh, my God! What's wrong with the brigadier in the end, to march eastward, the occupation of the west town? Oh, my god, this command can't be executed.

Doob Lieutenant: Military orders can't be disobeyed, you must do! Sir, joking is not allowed in the army, you can't hesitate! The soldiers of the whole company are waiting!

Lukasz: Shit! This command is obviously bullshit!

Doob Lieutenant: Sir, please pay attention to your words. In my opinion, there are only two views: the one is the view from the superior officer, and the other is the wrong view. Brigadier will never go wrong in our opinion of the junior officers, come on, make a decision!

Lukasz: Get out! You are trying to drive me mad! Double-dealer and self-dramatizing villain. I tell you, even if I die, you can't take my place yet.

(A soldier leads Svejk to come on.)

Soldier: Excuse me, Lukasz captain, your orderly Svejk missing several days came back.

Lukasz: Who? Who did you say?

Svejk: (come out from the back of the soldier, salute) Sir, the orderly Svejk finally find you!

Lukasz: (dizzy, and shook his body, then slump in a chair.) A few junior officers wipe his face with a wet towel. He points to Svejk with trembling fingers) You, you, you……

Svejk: Dear Captain, you'd better be able to control your mood, don't be so excited. I know you've been thinking of me. I was also missing the troops and you all the time these days when I left you! Look, I'm not fine and come back to your side again? We both are destined to stay together all our life, which is how to say in Chinese? Yes, it is fate. According to our views, this is God's plan.

Lukasz :(Look at the people around) Get out, don't come in any more! Svejk, don't go away! You see how I deal with you! You big jerk, idiot, stupid cow!

Svejk: yes, we are the single chat!

(Everyone leaves the stage.)

Lukasz: The people to be hanged will not be drowned! Idiot, why don't you die outside, why are you always badgering me. My god, I did what evil in the end in my previous life, and you have to be sent to torment me without end? No, no, I can't stand you anymore! I'm going to hang you, shoot you, stab you with a knife and split you with an ax!

Svejk: Sir, drink water, and keep calm. We don't talk whether you die or I live. Your anger is too big, which is not good for anyone. I'm your orderly, and ensure I'll die after you, I am always looking after you, serving you!

Lukasz: Shut up, the blockhead in the world. You don't serve as my orderly, and you are dreaming! Get out, I don't wish to see you any more, don't want to hear you say a word!

Svejk: Sir, I can't do that. I must obey orders, Colonel Shrader let me continue to do your orderly. Oh, I nearly forgot, this is his personal letter, which he let me bring to you, and everything is written plainly in the letter.

Lukasz : (hold a letter with one hand, and vigorously grab his hairs with the other hand) Virgin Mary, help me! I'm going to report to their superiors that I've got a new orderly Barron, though this guy is an idiot, scallywag!

Svejk: Forget it, sir! I am kinda silly, but never eat your snacks and sausage. Barron, everyone knows, as long as he sees anything to eat, everything is forgotten. His appetite is so big that even the lunch box and table can be swallowed.

Lukasz: It also doesn't work! You can't serve as my orderly any more! You asshole, keep up with me, I've encountered misfortunes even more than the cockroaches on the station. Why did you pull the emergency brake on the train to cause the accident? Why did you displease the general without hairs so that I was scolded? Why did you steal the Colonel's dog and then give it me so that I was shot almost? God, you own say how many you did like such bad things!

Svejk: Sir, I am a warm-hearted person, always want to try my best to share your sorrow. But I didn't do well all the time, and always make you angry. You can't completely blame me either!

Lukasz: Shut your dirty mouth! You look like an idiot! You are real or false in the end? Share concerns for me? You can really speak! I ask you, the last time I sent you to receive the young woman Mrs. Katie looking for me, how did you do? You actually fuck had sex with her, and dared to make the ephor' lover pregnant. You still dare to say to share concerns for me? Idiot!

Svejk: Sir, I have to explain a few words for this. I was completely in accordance with your orders! That day you said you were busy with work, let me explain to her. You said, to ask her whether she had some requirements, and try to satisfy her. She said she wanted to drink, I bought three bottles of wine; she wanted to smoke, I went to buy two packs of cigarettes for her; later she changed a transparent underwear and then asked me good or bad, I said "very good"; then she let me take off my pants to let her have a look ......

Lukasz: Shut up, mangy dog. Soldiers, put him into guardhouse three days, not allowed to drink or eat!

(The two soldiers come on, and Doob Lieutenant is subsequently coming. Svejk is grinning to salute Lukasz, and leaves with two soldiers.)

Doob Lieutenant: (glare at Svejk, and shook his fist) Bastard, you don't know me. I'm not so gentle and kind as Lukasz captain, and if you fell on my hands, I would make you cry, kneel down to beg for mercy!

Svejk: Yes, I was lucky!

(Svejk turns around and leaves.)

Lukasz: Dubrovnik Lieutenant, what's up?

Doob Lieutenant: Captain, a special train just moved into the train station. An old general was ordered to check the troops' civilization construction. I saw you were busy with work, being reprimandi̇ng Svejk, so I didn't bother you, and I accompanied the old general to visit our company on behalf of you.

Lukasz: Dubrovnik lieutenant, Currying favor with the leadership is your advantage. Such an opportunity couldn't

be given to others. So, did the old general have any
instructions?

Doob Lieutenant: Yes, Captain! He instructed that our soldiers
must strictly enforce the timetable, being at the dinner table,
sleep and toilet on time. Especially the last one, he thought
the public toilet was an important foundation to support the
Austrian victory. He didn't allow soldiers to relieve
themselves anywhere, because it wouldn't be hygienic. The
general checked the public toilets personally, and
considerately asked each soldier out of the toilet: "Did you
wipe it?" His attitude was very nice, not bureaucratic airs
at all, very approachable!

Lukasz: Shit! Dining and sleep on time, didn't you ask him
who gave us to supply for food, and where we could sleep? Our
rations have been ate up, did you report to him?

Doob Lieutenant: I didn't dare, we are always to show good
news, which is discipline. How could I dare to violate it?
Oh, the old general also suggested that we should send a person
responsible for writing the history of the company and the
history of the camp, in order that every victory we won and
soldiers and officers' heroic deeds were recorded detailedly.
He said: "No glorious history of the company, and then there
would be no brilliant history of the camp; no glorious history
of the camp, and then there would be no glorious history of
the brigade; no glorious history of the brigade, and then there
would no brilliaht history of the division……"

Lukasz: Shut up, up! No glorious history of the division, and
then there would be no glorious history of the troops. All
is nonsense, did we win once? Is there a soldier to want to
be a hero?

(Svejk comes on.)

Svejk: Sir, I want to be a hero!

Lukasz: You idiot, how dare you come out from the guardhouse?

Svejk: No, sir. I couldn't crowd. The guardhouse is too small, and it has been filled, even a mouse couldn't get into it, so they had to let me come back to wait. There are still a dozen people in front of me in the queue!

Lukasz: The good thing always happens to you shit.

Svejk: Thanks to you, let me have dumb luck!

Lukasz: Soldier!

(Two soldiers come on.)

Lukasz: I order you, to release a few bastards from the guardhouse and then put Svejk into it firstly! I don't believe I can't subdue you!

Svejk: Thank you for priority for me!

(An officer comes on.)

Officer: Mr. Captain, I just received a command from the brigade, let us set out to go to the north immediately by train.

Lukasz: Shit! Haven't you made a mistake? This is the terminus of the train, there is no railway ahead! (He knocks on the table with his fist) Notice troops assemble immediately, move forward on foot, to the north.

Svejk: Sir, should I go to guardhouse yet? Or you are waiting for me three days and then leave?

Lukasz: Get out! I'm going to send you to the trench on the front line, to watch you be blasted into meat!

Svejk: Well, let me go to the toilet, start off at once! (leave from the other side of the stage.)

"End"

"**Act VI**"

(Frontline. A simple post for the operations command, ruins. Lukasz captain, Doob lieutenant and a few officers are gesturing around a map, all talking at once. A few meters away, the recorder of the history of the camp, Malek is sitting on an ammunition box and writing the history of the camp.)

Lukasz : (Shout at a soldiers coming to report the situation) Come on, how about the front-line situation?

Soldier: Sir, the line of defense has been broken through!

Lukasz: Well, we finally broke through the defense. We are meritorious finally! Doob lieutenant, ask volunteers Malek for the record of this brilliant campaign in the history of the camp.

Soldier: Excuse me, sir, you got it wrong. It is that our defense has been broken through by the enemy! Fast run, no, fast retreat! Otherwise we all would be captured.

Lukasz: What? Idiot, even you couldn't speak clearly! I'm going to shoot you at once!

Doob Lieutenant: Mr. Captain, you'd better save a bullet. Let him hang himself!

Lukasz : (Shouting) Orderlies, Orderlies, damn, where are the orderlies?

Wonika: Sir, the orderly Svejk has disappeared, do you forget it? Before the troops set out, he said there was something wrong with his stomach, then hid in the woods to relieve himself, as a result, we never saw him again.

Lukasz: This beast must fall into the pit and be drowned! Haha, I feel so happy as soon as he has been drowned by stinking excrement!

(Svejk is dressed in a uniform of the Russian military and comes on, saluting.)

Svejk: Mr. Captain, orderly Svejk braved gunfire to report to you, I'm back!

Lukasz: My God, where do you come out, whose clothes are you dressed in? Come on, come on, stop him, don't let him approach me!

Doob Lieutenant: Son of bitch, Svejk! Standing at attention!

Svejk: (Stand at attention) Sir, children have no mother, it's a long story!

Lukasz: Cut off this shit, make it short.

Svejk: Well. On that day when our forces set out, my stomach felt uncomfortable suddenly, I could relieve myself on the spot. But I felt to some extent embarrassed in front of the buddies to take off my pants. You know I'm a shy person.

Doob Lieutenant: Damn, don't talk about something useless. Where did you run these days, and how have you been not seen all the time? Did you shit half a month?

Svejk: Lieutenant, please don't interrupt me. Have you forgotten that I carried you back from the brothel that day.

Doob Lieutenant: Shut up! If I'm angry, I'll make you cry.

Lukasz: Well, Dubrovnik Lieutenant, you go to the front-line trench, to encourage the brave soldiers grappling with an enemy!

Doob Lieutenant :(reluctantly) Yes!

(Doob lieutenant[3] leaves.)

Lukasz: Son of bitch, Svejk, please don't think I have no way to treat you! Come on, in the end how is it in the end?

Svejk: Captain, it was very simple. I was captured!

Lukasz: The Russian troops?

Svejk: Nope, it was our own troops that captured me.

Lukasz: Not allowed to play the mischief with me. Come on!

Svejk: That day I got into the woods, just squatted, I saw someone taking a bath in the lake ahead. That guy took off all the clothes. He was not afraid of catching a cold in such a cold day.

Lukasz: Don't talk rubbish, pick up the focus on that.

Svejk: Yes, come to the point immediately! I shouted at him, and he was so scared that he jumped out of the water and ran away. After relieving myself, I found a pile of clothes put on the side of the lake, which is just these clothes, which was left by that Russki. Then I tried it on, warmer and more suitable than my uniforms originally, so, I decided to use the new instead of the old. Unexpectedly, I was caught by our soldiers, who said that I was a Russian soldier, so I became the prisoner.

Lukasz: Why didn't you explain to them?

Svejk: Do you think it work? Is there anything can be explained clearly there days? For example, you should have been promoted to the captain, but how to explain? So, they were going to hang me later!

Lukasz: It should be actually done. Why haven't you been hanged? Well, you have to dirty my hands!

Svejk: The judge in the military court said last time he sentenced a prisoner to death by hanging, but can't be executed because no trees can be found in the desert. He also said that you wouldn't be so lucky today, here were trees everywhere. Later, another judge still verified with our regiment, and then the two judges had a dispute, have agreed to hang me, but the later insisted I should be released first, to catch a big fish, I do not know whether the big fish they was going to catch is you?

Lukasz: Damn, don't involve me, is there anything to do with me? You make trouble, don't pull me into it.

Svejk: Yes, sir. But the world has a common link, according to the logic of the judges, maybe someone would be hanged along with me.

(An officer comes on.)

Officer: Captain, the regiment notifies you immediately take part in a meeting.

Lukasz: Svejk, the matter between you and me is not finished yet, so I should find you after the meeting is over.

Svejk: Well, I'm waiting for you!

(Lukasz leases, and Svejk moves to the side of the camp volunteers Malek being writing the history.)

Svejk: Hi, man, you're historian Dr. Malek, right?

Malek: Hi, Svejk, I've heard your name!

Svejk: You flatter me. I'm just a soldier, providing the service for the captain, and loyal to the emperor, but you are a historian remaining immortal. Have you make many records about the history of our company and the camp, right?

Malek: Yes, Svejk, I have written a lot of achievements and victories of our camp. You know, I use a prophecy style of writing to write the history. Our camp was just moving from victory to victory.

Svejk: Oh, it sounds very interesting. Did you say that all things written actually never happened?

Malek: Yes. For example, this story I just wrote, our camp attacked a regiment of the enemy at night, each of us met an enemy, and exhausted all the effort to stab in his chest with

the bayonet, only to hear the crackling of broken ribs
everywhere. The limbs of the enemies falling sleeping twitched,
opening their eyes in a panic, bleeding from the corners of
the mouth, and can't shout, then finally legs were stretched,
and died! That's the end of the matter, and the victory belongs
to our camp. I still recorded one thing much greater: About
three months later, our battalion captured the Russian Tsar.
This story was so long that I'll tell you about it later. I
have to accumulate bit by bit some unique episodes of our
battalion during the combat, to compile some new terms of war.
I've thought of a plot, our officer, for example, a platoon
leader of the twelfth or the thirteenth company, his head was
blown off by the landmine of the enemy......
(Svejk is going to turn away.)
Malek: Svejk, wait. Can you tell me certain platoon leader's
name of the twelfth company?
Svejk: I know a man named Horska.
Malek: Well, it's him! The platoon leader Horska, his head
was blown off by the mine.
Svejk: I know how the head could be blown off by the landmine.
It should be reasonable that the feet were brown off.
Malek: None of your business. Anyway, I recorded like this.
His head was blown off, but the body was still moving forward,
and so well-placed, that a plane was shot down by one shot.
He is a great hero! The emperor was going to hold the
celebration for óur camp in the palace. You know, there are
hundreds of camps in Austria, only our camp got such a grand
prize. All the royal family, of course, including the Queen
and the Princess, as well as all ministers, attended the
celebration for our camp, how interesting!

Svejk: What you recorded were good things, it sounds excited.

Malek: Svejk, not simply good things. No sacrifice, it couldn't be successful, so the history of the camp can't be a series of victories. I have compiled forty-two victories like this. According to my notes, we had a lot of casualties as well!

Svejk: I'm curious, how did we sacrifice? (Another three soldiers come over.)

Malek : (turning over the note in his hand) For example, Barron, you often feel hungry. You look at this paragraph: you were blasted into the meat by the bomb from the enemy plane when eating Lukasz Captain's lunch.

Barron : (Distressed) Why could I die like this, you let me feed myself and then die, okay?

Malek: It has been already recorded. The history can't be distorted. Actually your death was as brave as Svejk's.

Svejk: How are you going to let me die?

Malek: Let me have a look, (turning over his notebook) It was found. Svejk, you look at it for yourself.

Svejk: You're still to help read!

Malek: Listen to me carefully: Svejk was seriously injured, dragged his broken legs, lying quietly beside the barbed wire. In the night, when the enemy searched the positions with the searchlight Svejk was found, and they thought Svejk were performing reconnaissance missions, then began to fire to Svejk. Svejk made a great contribution to the whole camp, because the enemy used all the ammunition that should be used to deal with a camp in the Svejk. Svejk's dismembered body was free to fly in the sky of the position with the smoke of the explosion......

Another two soldiers: About us, have you written?

Malek: Of course, the one is telephone operator Hotho Wonski.

Soldier A: It's me!

Malek: The other is the cook Yue Raida.

Soldier B: Right, right, right, both of us were really written into the history of the camp!

Malek: Close to me, gentlemen! (Say and turn over the note) Page 15, you both look, telephone operator Hotho Wonski and the cook Yue Raida sacrificed on September 3 together.

Two soldiers: How could it be so coincident?

Malek: You keep listening to me: the former risked his life to watch phone in the shelter, and stayed at the side of the phone three days and nights, no one came to replace; the latter, in the face of the outflank of the enemy, carried the pot filled with hot soup to the enemies, who scalded the shit out of them. They both were sacrificed bravely. When they sacrificed, both shouted: "Our company commander is long live! (raise heads) the Headquarters of the General Staff issued a citation specially for this, and called on all the soldiers to treat you as an example, learn from your courage and heroic spirit.

Svejk: Both of them were too spiritedness, simply psychotic! (Lukasz comes on.)

Lukasz :(flustered) Collection of all the soldiers.

Svejk: Excuse me, sir, should we have to set out?

Lukasz: Nothing, I don't have time to talk nonsense with you. Anyway, it's none of your business.

Svejk: Sir, I am your orderly, so I should go where you appear.

Lukasz: Get out of here, you are not my orderly. You are captured by our army.

Svejk: Sir, this is a serious matter. Since I joined in the

army, most of the time was taken to follow you.

Lukasz: It is not my fault, why didn't you put on the uniform of the Russian? (Shouting towards the distant) Doob lieutenant, Quartermaster Sergeant Wanica! Damn, all dead? I need help!

 (A few soldiers come on.)

Lukasz: Where are the other people, just you guys?

Soldier A: Sir, they have surrendered to the enemy, and only we remain.

Lukasz: Why didn't you run away?

Soldier B: Because my leg was blown off, I couldn't run.

Lukasz :(look at another soldier) How about you? Your legs were also broken?

Soldier C: Sir, my legs weren't broken. But I couldn't find a white cloth, so I had nothing to wave.

Lukasz: You're coward, stand at attention! I just received the indication from our superiors, let us put down our arms and surrender. But, Svejk, you are not allowed to surrender.

Svejk: Yes, sir!

Lukasz: Do you know why you can't surrender?

Svejk: No, sir.

Lukasz: You're a fool, an idiot! Because you are our prisoner, you are the Russian soldier!

Svejk: Sir, I am your orderly.

Lukasz: You're not my orderly, you are our prisoner! Do you understand?

Svejk:Yes, sir! I follow you, I am what you say I should be.

Lukasz: Well, we now are captives, I'm going to exchange me with you.

Svejk: I follow this order, obey the command.

Lukasz :(Sigh) Well, thank God, the war is over!

Svejk: There is a little pity, I thought we spent at least
fifteen years on the fight! Only four years, we had surrendered,
I'm ashamed of the emperor!
Lukasz: Svejk, on the eve of death you are talking nonsense!
If let the gendarmes heard, I followed you in trouble.
Svejk: Sir, don't worry. The gendarmes have surrendered!
(Guns sounds everywhere, Lukasz is scurrying round with his
head buried in by his hands. Svejk grasps him, and carries
him to escape. Everyone leaves.)

"End"

3

"Act Ⅶ "

(Two years after the end of the First World War. The "Bei Bei Man" pub in the town is still run by the boss Barry Horowitz after he was released from the prison, and his wife still helps him take care of the guests. The pub's business is significantly better than that during the war. At this point, there are five or six guests who are drinking, Barry Horowitz and his wife are busy filling the glass with wine for guests.)

Hasek:(Enter the pub and sit down, put the crutches away) Waiter, one beer! Come on!

Barry Horowitz :(tip his wife a wink) He is impatient as well. Come on, let him drink to go to hell!

Mrs. Barry Horowitz: I think you'd better go. He looks like a bad guy, ruder than the police!

Hasek: Up, up, my throat seems to smoke, wine, don't wait for the fire brigade to put out the fire!

Barry Horowitz :(limp) Your wine, sir, come on! Drink up and then start off!

Hasek: Off? Where? I'm not going anywhere, today I'm sitting here and not leave, to drink up all your wine in the pub! Hey, what's up with your legs......

Barry Horowitz: The Memorial left by the war!

Hasek: You also went to the front line? A hero!

Barry Horowitz: Not a hero, a prisoner. My legs were broken when I was in prison. You are?

Hasek :(take off his hat and fling it down on the desk) Mr. Barry Horowitz, you're son of bitch, can't you recognize me?

Barry Horowitz :(Perplexed) Oh, my God, my Lord, my Virgin Mary, you are Svejk, no, no, no, you're Mr. Hasek? My Angel

Sister, you did not die, you are still alive, you also drink after dying?

Hasek :(stand up and hug Barry Horowitz, and hit on the shoulders each other) Haha, you're still alive, I couldn't die!

Mrs. Barry Horowitz:(say and wipe tears with her apron) Mr. Hasek, you come back finally, I'm so happy!

Barry Horowitz: Well, don't be crying, you've seen Mr. Hasek, but not to attend his funeral. Come on, ladies and gentlemen, this is the famous Svejk, his real name is Hasek. Come on, everyone, it's my treat today, everybody enjoys drinking!

Hasek: Well, let's toast first, for the Republic!

Barry Horowitz: Shit, for ourselves! Svejk, I called you Svejk, right?

Hasek: OK, go ahead, whatever!

Barry Horowitz: Svejk, we have always thought you was dead these years, I didn't really expect to live to see you.

Hasek: Me too, I thought I can't see myself! The newspaper published the message about my death many times, that I was hanged, or that I fell into the pit and was drowned, or that I was shot. Hey, you know our news is never a real thing! Recently the newspaper also published an article to mourn for me, saying that I clashed with a group of seafarers because of being drunk, and was stabbed to death! Yesterday, I met the author writing the article to mourn in a pub, and he was so scared that he was near the brink of death. His face was pale, trembling, and his eyes riveted on me and asked: "Have you been to stay in Russia?" I said: "Yes, you finally recognize me. In an low-level restaurant of the Russian Odessa, I fought with a group of rude seamen drunk, as a result, I was stabbed by them. You also wrote an article to mourn me!" He asked me carefully with fear: "Can I help you? All fees, a total of fifty-five krone, are given to you, how about?" I replied:" I don't want money, just want to change another place and let you accompany me one night. " He asked:" Where? " I grasped his hand and said:" Go to the quiet cemeteries in the outskirts. "He was so scared that his hands and feet turn cold like ice, and get rid of me and ran, screaming all the way!

Barry Horowitz: Svejk, I feel uncomfortable as well. You couldn't be a ghost, right? God blesses me! You know, even your old maid Mrs. Miller also believes you've been dead, she still built a grave false in your backyard for you, in which your favorite dog was buried, and often gives new soil to your grave.

Hasek: Mrs. Miller is okay? I've been looking for her.

Mrs. Barry Horowitz: It's a pity, Mrs. Miller went into heaven six months ago! (Draw a cross)

Hasek: Oh, my God, how did she die?

Mrs. Barry Horowitz: Mrs. Miller was arrested when she sent you with the wheelchair to join in the army. The military court stood her trial, but because they were unable to find any evidence to condemn, she was sent to a concentration camp. After the war, she served the president of Domestic Labor Protection Association. At night, she rolled down from the stairs and died when she went to the basement to carry coal for cooking for the owner. Quite miserably, a seventy-year-old woman carried a big bag of coal and climbed up the stairs, it would be miracle if she didn't died!

Hasek: May her soul rest in peace!

"Haobingshuaike" cover one kind

Barry Horowitz: go, go, go, fill the glass with wine! Don't mention the sad things! Come on, let's drink! Alas, Svejk, how did you live these years, just as what is written in " Svejk "?

Hasek: More or less! At the end of the war, I became a prisoner, and then took part in the Soviet Red Army, joined the party, then served as a Mission political commissar, just simple like this.

Barry Horowitz: You're boasting, can you become a commissar? Kidding me!

Hasek: Yeah, yeah, I knew you wouldn't believe it, even sometimes I don't believe it, and I thought I had a dream! But the facts are facts, and these years, to tell the truth always is laughable.

Barry Horowitz: You return to Czechoslovakia this time, what do you plan to do?

Hasek: Currently I'm looking for a job! Now I'm ready to re-form a political party.

Barry Horowitz: What party?

Hasek: Before joining the army, I set up a party organization, the full name is "A small progressive party within the scope permitted by law," I'm going to re-form it, and I regard myself as the party chairman.

Barry Horowitz: The name is too interesting, how many members are there in the party?

Hasek: Currently[3] only me, you want to join?

Barry Horowitz: I? I'm rough, and never care about what fuck politics, I just sell beer.

Hasek: How about the Czech Republic and the past Austro-Hungarian Empire, which is better?

Barry Horowitz: More or less. The past officer is an officer now, and still enjoying life; the past humble person in the past are still living in the lower classes, still suffering. Hey, people like us, just live in peace, as long as no war, the police don't find fault, we are satisfied.

Hasek: You're right as well. Have you had the emperor's picture covered with feces of flies?

Barry Horowitz: Maybe. It has always been placed in the attic, and I guess it has been bit by the damn rats more or less.

Hasek: Haha, the era has been enlightened. If in the past years, you had to be sentenced to ten years in prison because of this sentence you said just now, maybe directly hanged. The emperor who was ate up by rats had a more serious sin than the one who was covered with feces of flies!

Barry Horowitz: Yeah, yeah, Mr. Hasek, I have a foul mouth, and will forget myself as soon as I see you. I never talk shit topic like this with others.

Hasek: Does the spy Schneider often come to the pub to eavesdrop on the customer's conversations?

Mrs. Barry Horowitz: Don't you know, that villain has been dead. He was killed by the mongrel dog you sold him, and ate. But, the new police officers of the republic often come here as well, and still constantly asking nearby residents' views on government.

Barry Horowitz: Come on, busy with your work, the old woman is talkative. Sir, the ordinary people like us don't really care about the national affairs, our priority is to make money, eat, and sleep.

Hasek: Man, I've got to tell you a few words more. Since the state power appeared, in all the history through the ages, you couldn't find half perfect, flawless state institution. On the contrary, in each country, there are always some guys unruly, and unsatisfied with the status quo. Man, I don't refer to you!

Barry Horowitz: I know, I know, I'm always satisfied with my status quo when born.

Hasek: Some people actually kept saying that our situation was terrible. We shouldn't think so. The newspaper said recently, half a million people were starved to death in Gansu Province of China, 800000 people were starved to death in Shaanxi Province. Did such things happen to the countries that had the import of the flour from China?

Barry Horowitz: You're right, we aren't starved to death.

Hasek: Our grocery store is filled with poultry meat, but residents complain that they are too expensive, and they simply can't afford. But some countries in the world actually have no beef, even if you have money, it can't be bought. In Southern Africa there is an Indian tribe where no one know what the sugar is like, but no one is suffering from the diabetes among our VIPs.

Mrs. Barry Horowitz: You're right, sir. We've got a customer who would like to drink beer with sugar, boring!

Hasek: In addition, compared with the authoritarian countries, we are too free! A few countries, I don't mention their name, where people are[3] caught, killed and cut the head casually, but now our heads are still on our necks?

Barry Horowitz: Thank you, our king, keep my fool head.

Hasek: Moreover, I think recently a very unhealthy tendency is growing in the life of our republic, if its spread can't be controlled, it will destroy the harmony and happiness in the future. This trend stems from jealousy that people are not always willing to see others better than their own! For example, some people always complain about the high-income officer, as long as they heard the Minister of Finance and the Governor of the Bank has been a huge increase in salary, they vent their discontent, clamoring to get a raise for themselves, completely regardless of our country being in the economic crisis. They still said, Minister's got a mansion, why does he still go to the villa to stay with his family, how could he speak out these words?

Barry Horowitz: He is so lucky natively!

Hasek: A few days ago, a citizen said to me: "an officer is coming and going by car, but I don't even have no money to take the tram." I really wanted to teach him a lesson: "No fuss, you can't even have no money to take the tram, of course, no money to take a car! A citizen can't feel jealous because you don't afford to the fees of taking a car, right? Everyone should have morality, only in this way can we develop a healthy and national spirit!

Customer A: This gentleman speaks out what we want to say in hearts, I just rely on my legs to walk, not even take the tram.

Customer B: Yes, I also save the fare in order that I have money to drink!

Customer C: Mr. Hasek, there are some workers who are jealous of our boss in our plant, saying that "his life is a lot better than we are, and what we earn in the whole year is less than one-tenth of his spending. " Sir, you're knowledgeable, do you think this sentence is right?

Hasek: It's wrong, completely wrong. Workers should have a

kind of a noble mind than the jealousy, that is, labor is glorious, and happily labor! The worker shouldn't measure everything by money, and he should be an idealist, not haggle over every ounce, but must be willing to experience happiness in hard labor, and contented in poverty and devoted to things spiritual!

Barry Horowitz :(lead to applaud) Mr. Hasek, you just said that you have been a political commissar in the Red Army of Russia, and now I believe it, your consciousness ideologically is indeed higher than ours.

Mrs. Barry Horowitz: Mr. Hasek, I think you are more and more like Svejk, what you said is always irony.

Customer A: Maybe his head was damaged by the shells when joining the fight.

Hasek: My friends, if you think what I said made sense, then I'll write them down, ready to publish it on the "People's Political News", and suggest that this article be added into the textbooks, with my heartfelt words to teach students, and I am willing not to get royalties completely. Oh, it is late, and I'm going to the Social Committee for Relief, to find a job to maintain livelihoods firstly. Barry Horowitz, thank you for your beer. Friends, goodbye!

Everyone: Goodbye!

"End"

3

"Act VIII"

(Social Committee for Relief, in the office of the President,
who are sitting at the desk, a lady wearing fashionably is
nestled in his arms, and put candy into his mouth. Hasek stands
at the doorway and coughs twice.)

President: Who? Why does it appear in this time!

Hasek: It's me, Hasek, president.

Lady: Shit, leave him alone!

President: Hush, keep quiet. (Push her, tidy up clothes, and
spit out candy, then clear his throat.) Come on in!

Hasek: Mr. President, I bother you!

President: Oh, it was my dear, Mr. Hasek, hi, hi! Oh, (turn
to the lady) Young lady, you go back firstly, for what you
said, we can study carefully! (Close to young lady's ear)
Tonight we see in the old place! (Secretly pat on young lady's
ass) Ah, dear, Mr. Hasek, sit down, sit down! I feel, to call
you Svejk appears to be more intimate. You know, I just watched
the drama "Svejk". It's so really funny that my belly nearly
burst, thanks to my belt, which is made of fine leather, very
strong, so that I can keep my noble stomach.

Hasek: Thank you!

President: Oops, simply ridiculous. Is there really this idiot
like Svejk in life? I think he pretends to be fool, with a
unique perspective of a fool to measure, criticize and mock
us.

Hasek: Mr. President, I want you ......

President: Please wait, I want to tell you, I've heard Lukasz
Captain is running the business on hops with his former lover's
husband together at the end of the war, and exports hops to

Italy, France, Britain and Russia, made a fortune.

Hasek: I know Lukasz's lover, Mrs. Katie. I have seen her!

President: Hey, I think of it. Did she have sex with Svejk?

Hasek: Maybe!

President: Mr. Hasek, maybe you don't know it, I'm related to Doob lieutenant to some extent. He was a language teacher originally in a high school, and treated his students as prisoners, liked to use high-flown words, but did some shady and indecent actions secretly. It is said that, after defecting to the Russians, he was shot because of seducing the general's wife and daughter at the same time. As for Katz father who said he could slap three flies, he wrote an open letter to scold you recently, and would sort you, saying you destroyed his reputation. However, he couldn't sort you, because he can be drunk twenty-four hours a day.

Hasek: Mr. President, I have got to interrupt you. Because you busy, I don't want to take up more of your time.

President: No, no, no, Mr. Hasek, I'm bored, and going to talk about Svejk's anecdotes with you.

Hasek: Sorry, sir, I have no interest in it, just want to ask the social committee for relief for the introduction of a job for me.

President: Well, it is difficult for me. I remember the last time you came here, I have made it clear to explain. I really like you, admire you, but you know, this feeling can't replace the policy, I work with emotion, but not emotionally. The power is given to me by the citizens, so I can't abuse my power.

Hasek: Sir, just introduce a job to me, it is the responsibility of the Committee for Relief. How is the abuse of power?

President: Yeah, yeah, there are indeed the obligations to

recommend and introduce a job, but you are neither a thief,
drunkard, orphan, robber or slip girl, nor homeless cat and
dog or cattle suffering, you don't meet requirements. How can
I do? I'm not an official who violates law and discipline.

Hasek: But I'm disabled!

President: We can't help the disabled.

Hasek: Mr. President, you mean, let me steal and rob, or become
a pet dog?

President: I don't mean that. Well, you just reminded of me.
I'll give you an idea, but you can't tell others. Okay? You'd
better go to the bar and fill your stomach with plenty of wine,
then take advantage of alcohol, go to ......

Hasek: Sir, I don't even afford to food, how can I have the
money to drink?

President: En, so well ...... I'll make an exception today,
ready to sacrifice, and to lend you a bottle of spirits -
whiskey. You drink it up, then buy one to me later. (He pulls
out a bottle of wine under the desk, and puts it in front of
Hasek) You drink it up, and then down the stairs, turn right,
and the building, on the left besides the main street at the
second intersection, is Prague City Police Department, as long
as you break into it with the alcohol, and break something
like glass, I guarantee you will get meals a month.

Hasek :(Take over the bottle, and drink it up) Sir, have I
got to break the police?

President :(Nods) Yeah, yeah.

Hasek: Why to detour? Break here!

President:(Hurriedly stand up to block) No, no, no, Mr. Hasek,
please control your emotions!

(Hasek throws the bottle onto the ground, and picks up the

cup, flower pots, folders to throw around, then turns round
and raises the chair to throw towards the President.

President:(Shout) Help! I need help!

"End"

Socrates

Characters

Socrates: Ancient Greek philosopher, born in 469 BC, which was the golden age of Athens Pericles ruled, and sentenced to death by Athens court in 399 BC in the name of introducing a new God and corrupting the Athenian youths' thoughts

Critto: Socrates' friend

Phaedo: Socrates' students. Socrates talked with him before dying, which was recorded in the Dialogues of Plato, namely, "Phaedo".

Aristophanes: Early ancient Greek comedist, the Athenian citizen.

Meletus: A poet in Athens, the leader of three people prosecuted Socrates.

Diotima: A priestess in the Greek Mantinea, who had told the truth about love to Socrates.

Koscipa: Socrates's wife.

Agathon: A tragic poet in Athens

Koehler Weng: A General in Athens

Ecualardy: Socrates' student

Shoemaker, carpenter, pastries providers, judges, several jurors, jailor, and bailiff, Socrates' sons, as well as several people

3

(Opening words)

(Phaedo is staggering on the stage, trudge, with exhaustion on his face. He suddenly falls down when passing two young men. The young men hurriedly come forward to prop him up, and took out a kettle to give him water.)

Youth A: Friend, who are you?

Youth B: Where are you from, and where will you go?

Phaedo: (slowly wake up, and talk slowly and feebly) I seemed to hear a philosophical question: Who are you, and where are you from and where to go? Since the teacher's death, no one has raised such questions for a long time.

Youth A: Haha, you are the Socrates' student Phaedo, right?

Phaedo: Yes, I came from Athens and am going to Foley. Suffering from hunger and starvation along the way, I actually fell down. You must have already known that Socrates was executed.

Youth B: We have heard, what a pity! Everyone said, this is an injustice that never happened. But we do not know the details, you can tell us about it!

Youth A: Yes! In fact, these days we are expecting you, we heard that since Socrates died, you've been wandering around, to tell the story about him.

Youth B: Excuse me, when Socrates was put to death, did you go with him?

Phaedo: Yes, I was near him.

(Ecualardy comes[3] on the stage.)

Ecualardy: So, what did the teacher said at last, and how was he in the face of death?

Phaedo: Do you know the trial process?

Ecualardy: Someone has told us, but we felt very surprised,

because from the end of the trial to the execution of the death penalty, they were separated for a very long time, what happened to him on earth?

Phaedo: That was a fortunate coincidence, on the day before the trial, Athenians just put a basket of flowers on the stern of the ship going to Delos.

Ecualardy: What kind of ship?

Phaedo: According to the legend, this ship had saved the lives of the Athenians, in order to repay, the Athenians had promised Apollo that they would go to Delos to worship each year. Until today they are fulfilling their promise. During the worship, Athens must be kept clean, and not allow to sentence to death overtly. Socrates's trial is the time to start the worship ceremony, so Socrates was waiting for so long in prison.

Ecualardy: But Phaedo, how about the teacher in the end, what did he say, what did he do and who were together with him, and did the prison guards prevent Socrates relatives and friends to visit?

Phaedo: Prison officials did not prevent. His wife and sons, as well as a lot of friends, accompanied him. Socrates was very calm and serene when he died.

Ecualardy: If you do not hurry on your journey, please tell us the story about Socrates in details now.

Phaedo: No, I'm not anxious to go. I'll tell you the truth. For me, there is nothing more meaningful in the world than telling the story about Socrates.

Ecualardy: Great, Phaedo, we share the same feeling with you, no matter now or in the future, the philosophy will be necessary for the human spirit, and Socrates' philosophy will illuminate our future.

"Act I"

(The lighting begins to rise, and the music starts. A person wearing an overcoat and big hat comes onto the stage from the auditorium, perform the ceremony of the dim and gloomy shape on the stage, to show opposition to Socrates. The lighting gradually disappears.)

(The lighting doesn't appear, music and laughter starts first. The lighting appears, there are three young people performing on the stage, surrounded by three to five people, including Meletus and Aristophanes.)

Onlooker A: Squat down again, Squat down again.

Onlooker B: Stick up his ass, well, well, well, keep rising! Look, Mr. Socrates is watching the astronomical phenomena!

Onlooker C: Yes, right, right! Keep going up! You would look farther. Do you see Zeus? What does he look like?

(The young onlookers are laughing and point to young people performing, while the performers are also laughing and show mischievous expressions and gestures to fit.)

Performer A: What is Zeus? Don't speak foolishly, Zeus does not exist.

Performer B: Right! Dad, Zeus does not exist.

Performer C: Is the rain not Zeus' urine, and is the thunder not Zeus' fart?

Performer B: Hum! Well, isn't it, Mr. Socrates?

Onlooker A: Look, he is a fool student, haha! (Everyone is laughing)

Onlooker B: Come on, hurry up to tell us, omniscient Socrates!

Performer A: The rain is naturally from the cloud god, because there is no cloud, there is no rain. The thunder is a sound generated from the collision of the clouds.

Performer B: Yes! Dad, you heard, everything is done by the cloud god!

Performer A: You are a good apprentice, pray to the cloud god with your father! I entered to get some sleep.

Onlooker C: Pretend to sleep quickly! (Performer A cooperates with them and falls asleep on the stage)

Performer A: Oh, my son, you go fast to kill Socrates with me! It is him who lied to you and me!

Performer B: But I do not want to hurt my teacher.

Performer C: You should respect the ancestors' Zeus.

Performer B: (say to the audience) we heard what he said about the ancestors' Zeus. (Said to his father) You're an old fogy. Where is Zeus? !

Performer C: He exists!

Performer B: You are off your head, and talk to yourself here! (Next act)

Performer C: Servants, come here! Carry the ladder and ax! (The young performers and onlookers played together, Meletus and Aristophanes sat aside and smilingly looked. Phaedo came on the stage, standing aside and watching.)

Performer C: Pull down his roof! Give me a torch, to burn him!

Performer A: (Came from the back of the stage) Ah, who burns our house?

Performer C: The one deceived by you.

Performer A: Oh, [3]bad luck, I am going to suffocate! Oh, bad luck, I am going to be burned to death!

Performer C: Why did you insult the gods! Servants, go to hit him! There are too many reasons that he can be beaten, especially because he blasphemed the gods.

(Phaedo was very angry when seeing here, and went to the center
of the stage.)

Phaedo: Stop! Why did you blaspheme my teacher? !

Performer A: We perform, it is Socrates in the drama. (There
are a few people repeating what he said together)

Meletus: Dear, Phaedo, we pay tribute to the master's work!
But you did not know, in yesterday's Dionysian drama contest,
Mr. Aristophanes' work has won applause from the audience!

Aristophanes: Oh, really? My drama is praised by the audience
every year, but never wins a prize.

Meletus: Today your "cloud", I'm sure it could get the first
prize.

Phaedo: (turn to Aristophanes) Aristophanes, what do you mean?
Why do you blaspheme my teacher? !

Aristophanes: Who can be stupid like you to take seriously
the trick in the drama!

(Phaedo is about to speak, and Socrates went on. The scene
was quiet, and all the people stood one after another and said
hello to Socrates.)

Socrates: What Aristophanes said is right. Phaedo, why do you
carry on fierce arguments for such a false issue on sunny days?

Phaedo: But how can Aristophanes describe you as sophist to
blaspheme gods? We all know that you are a wise man who knows
everything.

Socrates: I am not omniscient, on the contrary, I know I do
not know everything, so it is not that ignorant.

Aristophanes : (enthusiastic applause) the great and wise man
is going to give a speech again. Your next statement will be
my creative material of next comedy.

(Meletus discusses something with the youths performing before, Meletus walks up to Socrates.)

Meletus: Mr. Socrates, I want to talk to you. There are many questions puzzling and even dizzying me.

Socrates: Wait, do you feel dizzy at this moment?

Meletus: Yes.

Socrates: That's right, this feeling is the beginning of philosophy. Wisdom is produced in confusion. Of course, if it is because of the strong sunlight causing heat stroke, that is a medical problem, you can go to see a doctor.

Meletus: No, no, I'm not heatstroke, it is the confusion in my heart. Dear sir, I often think about the truth, virtue, courage, justice, love and friendship and other topics, I really wish to get your advice!

Socrates: Your confusion is also my confusion. What we can only do is to find ourselves in mutual dialogue and conversation. Know yourself, there is nothing more fundamental, more important and more difficult than that. My mission is to work with you to explore the truth, rather than act as a condescending prophet, to convey the issues that need to be explored as a conclusion to the unknown, if so, it is not a good education.

Meletus: But I do not have the ability to find the answer, Mr. Socrates! Thinking made me confused and painful, but beyond that, I found nothing.

Socrates: This is the throes before labor, because you are "pregnant".

Phaedo: Teacher, can't you see it? He's a genuine man! (All the youths are laughing)

Socrates: My eyes can completely tell the difference between male and female countenance. I just made an analogy. He is not empty, but already pregnant with the seed of truth, and waiting the delivery. A new life will be born in the throes. My mother was a midwife with superb skills, I inherited her skills, and clearly check out what produced in your heart is true or false in the end. God let me play the midwife of man's wisdom, but I can't produce. As people accuse me of that, "Socrates can only ask questions, but can't give answers. Yes, they're right, delivery is the will of God, and is also Socrates's duty. I can't "produce", but personally meet many new lives.

Meletus: Socrates, I do not understand yet, if you do not draw conclusions, how can I get the new knowledge?

Socrates: It's entirely feasible, don't treat me as a man who knows the answer, please. Because I do not know, I am about to talk to you together, in order to explore the truth. In fact, all the answers are given by yourself. For example, what is virtue?

Phaedo: I think virtue is ......

Socrates: Think carefully before answering.

Performer A: I think, sincerity and faithfulness, not to deceive others is virtue.

Socrates: I totally agree. But why did we try our best to deceive the enemy when fighting with the enemy?

Phaedo: To deceive the enemy is possible, but you can't deceive our own people. [3]

Socrates: I agree with you. But when our army was surrounded by the enemy, in order to boost morale, the general deceived soldier and said reinforcements had arrived, we tried our best to break out the encirclement, as a result, we won the battle.

Is this deception not a virtue?

Performer B: Socrates, what you say is at war, out of frustration. In everyday life, such deception is immoral.

Socrates: Really? If your child is sick, but refused to take medicine, as a father, you said it was delicious, sweet, cheat your kid to take medicine, which is a virtue?

Performer C: Socrates, it is certainly not against the moral!

Performer A: So, not to deceive people is a virtue, and to cheat others is a virtue?

Meletus: Whether to deceive people or not is not the standard of the virtue. It depends on whether he knows what is virtue. Right, Mr. Socrates?

Socrates: Thank you, you make me understand what virtue is. Now I assure you, I am not to refute you, but because I want to find out the problem. The truth is more important than the face. You said, is it a good deed to discover the truth of things for all mankind?

Meletus: Yes, Socrates, of course, it is a good deed.

Socrates: So, lovely sir, we should be happy. Not dejected, or angry. You and I do not care who wins the debate, but to seek and prove, you can refute me Socrates, but can not refute the truth.

Phaedo: Right!

Socrates: Only smart people can really understand himself. He can not only investigate what he knows or what he does not know, but also to understand what other people know. Some people either think they know some things but actually not know, or they do not know some things, but think they know something they do not know in fact. This is the wisdom, temperance and self-understanding, because one person must

know what they know, and know what they do not know. This is
what you mean?

Meletus: Yes. But, Mr. Socrates, your statements sound like
what everyone said, like a tongue twister. You were just as
a sophist in Mr. Aristophanes' play just now.

Socrates: Tongue twister uses "difficult language" to express
"difficulty in language", this is also a skill, which can be
got by studying. Studying is not only the youths' business,
I also need to constantly study. My friends, I believe that
each of us should find the best teachers for ourselves in our
life, including those older people, do not give up the search
for truth because you are older. The famous poet Homer said,
"Shyness is not a good moral character for people begging",
feeling unashamed to ask others for advice should be learners'
attitude.

(A woman's shouts appears from the theater outside: "Socrates,
go home for dinner!)

Aristophanes: Socrates, that is your wife's voice. Hurry up,
go home for dinner!

Socrates: Women are always like this, you can imagine it!
(Koscipa played.)

Koscipa: (hurry onto the stage, angrily one hand puts on her
waist and the other hand points to Socrates's nose) Do you
remember you have a family yet? Do you know you have married?

Phaedo: A famous philosopher must have a wife like a bitch
in his family. Teacher, what you said is right.

Socrates : (in the face of Koscipa) they all think this sentence
is my saying, in fact, I did not say that.

Koscipa: You are only aware of baloney and chatting in the street every day, and you will get flamed sooner or later! (Faced with Meletus) Do not believe his nonsense, "know yourself", you ask him whether he knows what his name yet? Hum, he will be unlucky one day!

Socrates: (turn to the audience and shrug, helplessly spread out his hands) what did I say just now, the woman is just like this! War and philosophy require women to walk away. Come on, I would fill the stomach first!

(Socrates, Koscipa and Phaedo go away together.)

Onlooker A: Did Mr. Socrates say clearly what virtue was just now?

Performer A: Mr. Socrates seems to prefer a debate with young people to giving the answers to problems.

Meletus: Stop this nonsense, Mr. Socrates is the world's smartest man, and we can't understand his wisdom in a moment yet.

Onlooker B: I do not understand, no cheat is a virtue, and deception is a virtue either? Oh, I was completely confused by it.

Performer C: Is not that sophistry?

Onlooker B: How could it, everyone says Mr. Socrates is the guide of Athens' youths!

Performer C: I ask you, is it important to solve the problem or manufacture issues?

(The young onlookers are speechless, looking at each other.)

Meletus: Think carefully, it is indeed more important to solve the problems, Mr. Socrates does not mislead the youth! ...... Impossible, impossible, how could he make such a mistake?

Performer C: I don't think so, Socrates was just bluffing,

that's all.

(Aristophanes feels the scene is awkward, gets up and wants to go.)

Meletus: how can you say that? I think Mr. Aristophanes should know this problem best.

Aristophanes: I'm just a poet, and do not understand things about philosophy well.

Performer B: (came to Aristophanes) Mr. Aristophanes, we quite admire your ability to have an insight into popular feeling!

Performer C: Yes, Mr. Socrates was shaped vividly in the "cloud" by you, and presumably you must understand what kind of man Mr. Socrates is well, right?

Aristophanes: As I just told Phaedo, only a fool would take seriously things in the play!

Performer C: that's must have a prototype in life, sir.

Aristophanes: I also wrote the consul, Mr. Pericles, General Koehler Weng in my drama before! Do you think the General Koehler Weng was also a clown like that in my play?

 (Three young performers look at each other, dumbfound, Meletus approached.)

Meletus: Let General Koehler Weng do our leader, which is God's grace to us.

Aristophanes: Oh? Whether this is God's grace to us, or to his own, it is difficult to say.

Meletus: Now we have the current orders in Athens, is it because God gave General Koehler Weng extraordinary wisdom and character?

Aristophanes: Oh, yes? Presumably the audience has discovered this in my play, or else they would not laugh.

Meletus: Mr. Aristophanes, all of us understand your banter, and respect gods, and support General Koehler Weng best like you.

Aristophanes: Ah, Mr. Meletus, if you have nothing, I will go first.

(Aristophanes turns and leaves the scene, but stops by Meletus)

Meletus: Mr. Aristophanes, please hear me out, the integrity and courage reflected in yesterday's play was very admiring, I think you are the model of Athens' citizen, I'm sure you will come forward for justice.

(Aristophanes keeps silent, Meletus continues.)

Meletus: But now there is a person, relied on a little eloquence to stir up trouble every day, to confuse the youth, carrying on the spread of blasphemous thoughts in the city. But he sees himself as the most intelligent person in the world, I think, this clever man should do something clever.

Aristophanes: Oh? I am afraid that untalented people always want to do what the wise man can do.

(Aristophanes leaves off the stage, the light closes.)

"End"

3

"Act II"

(The lighting is rising, Socrates' home.)

Koscipa: Stand up!

(The lighting rises, Koscipa and Socrates stand.)

Koscipa: I allow you to sit down to eat ? !

Socrates: I have discussed with those young people for a long time, and I have been hungry.

(Koscipa went into the kitchen, carried a tray and came out.)

Koscipa: Ah, they just talked, but not to provide the meal.

Socrates: It is the family meal that is delicious.

(Kiscipa rolls her eyes, Socrates is going to sit.)

(Koscipa puts dish on the table.)

Koscipa: Up! (Socrates immediately stands up) I did not allow you to sit down yet!

Socrates: If we are not to eat, the food will become cold.

 (Socrates sits down to eat.)

Koscipa: Why didn't you go back early? You only know to say, say, say all day long, it can be as food to eat?! You talk ceaselessly outside, but become dumb when going home.

(Socrates bends his head to eat, Koscipa picks up the sewing basket on the table and sewed clothes.)

Koscipa: You always talk about philosophy, the philosophy is to make you full, or allow you to get rich? The wise men put a stall in the square, blah, blah, blah, gold coins come into their pocket. But, you not only can't earn money, but also very anxious to lose money to make people listen to you.

Socrates: the fun philosophically, thinking happiness can not be measured by money. (To say) Well, you will never understand even if I tell you.

(Koscipa takes the bowl away.)

Koscipa: Well, well, well, you go to enjoy it! The enjoyment philosophically is in comparison with the roast beef!

 (Socrates is going to take the bowl back.)

Koscipa: Well, you, the great philosopher, tell me how much money this veal is! And fennel beans and bean soup?

Socrates: If talking about philosophy, I'm good at it; but to calculate the price, you're good at it. If you were to talk about philosophy, and I went to the market to buy vegetables, wouldn't it be in great confusion?

(Koscipa puts the bowl back on the table.)

Koscipa: Nothing can block your mouth.

Socrates: You're wrong. The only way to block my mouth is the roast beef you cook.

Koscipa: All right, you seem to lose your soul to go to the square all day long, and go with your students together, keep asking them this or that question. You argue with others day by day, what do you want to get?! And look at the bad friends, Mr. Aristophanes wrote a play, and described you were crazy and a liar. Our neighbors were laughing at me, you make me how to be faced with them? !

Socrates: Really? Aristophanes wrote a drama with irony about me, which made my wife uncomfortable. This is really an interesting phenomenon. Why do you think you are not glorious?

Koscipa: Okay, okay, please not deal with me as you ask your students. I still have work to do, no time to prattle.

(Koscipa cleans the bowls and goes off the stage, and Socrates also stands up after dinner and is going to leave.)

Koscipa: Are you going to the square again?

 (Koscipa steps forward to grasp Socrates.)

Koscipa: I don't allow you to go!

Socrates: Why?

Koscipa: Can't you see? Recently there are rumors regarding you everywhere. Quite a few people are talking about you surreptitiously. You don't go out as soon as possible, and talk less!

Socrates: What was they able to talk about me? I neither have ambitions in politics, nor care about politics. Some people like fishing, some people like meditation, I do not have any other hobbies, just like sharing the enjoyment of debate and thinking. If you don't allow me to enjoy this fun, I might as well die.

(Koscipa moves a chair and places it in front of Socrates.)

Koscipa: I do not know the great truth, anyway, I don't allow you to go to the square. Other wise men can get the money when they speak. But it is not a good business when you speak. I finally see you act as an officer, and let you review a case--- how many people died in that naval battle, I hate those officers --- but you spoke in a bureaucratic tone, fair, justice, and wanted to acquit the panjandrums.

Socrates: I'd like to ask, why do you want to sentence them to death, I sentenced them ......

Koscipa: Don't interrupt me, I don't want to argue with you. Do you know how many people you offend because of that? I had a month not to dare to go to the market. Fortunately, you were dismissed later![3] If you really released them, we would have to take your sons to move. You often go on the square all day to say the moon is a mass of soil, the sun is a fire. Oh, my God, like such words, you also dare speak casually, if it is heard by someone and then spread, I and the kids will have to follow you to fall on evil days. Anyway, don't follow what a woman says, suffer losses immediately. I advise you to cherish life, and keep away from the philosophy.

Socrates: So, do you believe the moon is a mass of soil, the sun is a fire?

(Koscipa looks curiously at Socrates, and shakes her head.)

Koscipa: Our sun is the Apollo's incarnation.

Socrates: Then I have a way to let you see the moon is a mass of soil and the sun is a fire, do you believe me?

Koscipa: Don't you go out?

Socrates: Today I am not out.

(Koscipa happily hugs Socrates. Both of them go off the stage.)

"End"

3

"Act Ⅲ"

(Koehler Weng appeared on the back area of the stage, and moved towards Meletus.)

Koehler Weng: Do you think he was crazy?

Meletus: Without a doubt. He does not want to work, lingers idly in the street all day, talks at random with young people, bringing destabilizing factors to our life.

Koehler Weng: How long is there no rain?

Meletus:(not rise) Presumably God is annoyed now.

Koehler Weng: Hey, why is God annoyed?

Meletus: No doubt, because he has always trumped up what he called a new god, meanwhile, he does not believe the original God. He is also surrounded by a lot of people who do not believe in God. The comic poet Aristophanes..….

Koehler Weng: Oh, I know, his "Arcana" seemed to win a prize, to require us to reconcile with the Spartans?

Meletus: It is him.

Koehler Weng: he is really a good poet!

Meletus: But in his play he portrayed Zeus as a rogue.

(Koehler Weng doesn't speak.)

Meletus: And, include some officials who betrayed our Athens, they were Socrates' students. Haven't you forgotten these?

Koehler Weng: Do you think Socrates is a dangerous man?

Meletus: Obviously. Mr. Anytus has been already dissatisfied with his son to go with Socrates all day long. As a result, this morning, his son actually contradicted him for a trivial matter, and laughed at his ignorance. This morning Mr. Anytus went to look for Socrates to "seek an explanation", as a result, Socrates humiliated Mr. Anytus in front of all the people on the square. The whole Athens is not really in his eyes!

Koehler Weng: That arrogant guy!

Meletus: If going on like this, the slaves would revolt against their owner, son would humiliate his father, his wife would contradict her husband, and the Athenian civilization and justice we want to maintain will be destroyed totally!

Koehler Weng: Do you think how to deal?

Meletus: At least he should not live in this city again.

Koehler Weng: If he is willing to appropriately do few remarks, I think it is an acceptable solution. As for the method, well, it can be eclectic.

Meletus: I think I've got a good idea.

"End"

3

(Celebrate the feast. Socrates and others sat around the table, the crowd appearing on the Scene II also sat around the table. After a few glasses of wine, everyone was drunk.)

Aristophanes: Dear friends, come on, let us raise a glass to celebrate the Agathon won the first prize in this drama contest, cheers!

Agathon: Oh, thank you, dear Aristophanes! Hopefully one day I can write a masterpiece like your "Arcana".

Aristophanes: Absolutely! What you need is some courage and cheek. Really, at that time, when "Arcana" was on show, I thought Euripides was certainly furious. But I do not care, the tragedy should have the characteristic of a tragedy, dignified, elegant, noble. I don't bear he put all the junk into the tragedy, wordy, bitter, and howling. I wrote heartily, and the audiences were also very happy!

Agathon: You know, what I appreciate is more than that! You can bluntly criticize the Athenians confused and fanatical patriotism, and only you can do it.

Aristophanes: Ah, I've been ready to meet the rotten eggs! In my play I can satirize and mock our citizens heartily! I did not expect everyone would like that play, and they awarded it a prize! Sometimes the mood of the audience is really elusive!

Phaedo: But, this time your "cloud"[3] did not win, which make us all surprised!

Aristophanes: This time I just missed a bit of luck, that's all.

Socrates: I think this is a very good play, and I myself also laughed a lot of times! (In the face of Aristophanes) you were pulling my leg in the theater, making me feel like being among a lot of good friends. But, if you describe me in the next play, can you make my image not so funny? My wife is upset by your play!

Phaedo: Absolutely! Your wife's temper is very irritable!

 (The crowd are talking about it mirthfully.)

Agathon: Dear friends, I propose that this cup of wine should be offered respectfully to Eros! Thank Eros and Aphrodite for guiding poets to offer the wonderful verse to the audience.

Socrates: Well, Agathon, I agree with your proposal. Those wonderful poems are not written by people, but God's works. The poet is the God's spokesman, and God is attached to the poets and dominates them. I have a toast with you, and also with God, for your wonderful work, Cheers!

Agathon: Love makes us crazy, just as wine is intoxicating, let me dizzy. The one, without love, can keep a cool head. I want to keep sober, but longing for love. Water is no substitute for wine, have a drink again!

Socrates: Lovely Agathon, don't be afraid of craziness, the craziness of love is not a sin. The conscious is not more commendable than the passionate. The craziness of love is a gift of Gods. It is the great gift God gives.

Phaedo: Teacher is right! Ah, invisible wings of love and soul can bring the heavy stuff to fly to the sky!

Aristophanes: Well, Socrates, I follow you, I intend to use a new way to praise Eros. I am sure that human beings haven't realized the power of love at all. If we knew what love is, the most solemn and most magnificent halls and altars would be built for Eros, and the most solemn ceremonies would be held!

Socrates: No, no, no, respected King of Comedy Aristophanes! I think, you are kidding, to praise Cupid's does not require massive construction and waste of resources! I have said, there are two kinds of commitments, one is to express with behavior and the other is with words. The noble language is both a memorial and to crown the noble acts.

Agathon: So, Mr. Socrates, what is love in the end?

Socrates: On this issue, we can ask Mrs. Diotima, for love, who has many insights. My dear Diotima, please tell us: What is love?

Diotima: Dear Socrates, in fact, you know better than me, love is a thing between mortal and immortal.

Agathon: What do you mean?

Diotima: It is a very powerful wizard. Elves are between God and man. It is neither mortal, nor immortal, because it has many variations within a day, sometimes vibrant, sometimes dejected. And love must be the devotee of wisdom.

Socrates: Dear Mrs., what you said is very good! Can I understand love is a kind of love for beautiful things?

Phaedo: Right! For example, I love the beautiful girl.

Diotima: Or it can be said that it is a kind of love for beautiful and good things.

Socrates: Your interpretation is more accurate.

Diotima: we all want to turn good things into our own.

Socrates: Yes. [3]

Diotima: by making good things become our own, what will we get?

Socrates: I can answer simply to this question: He will get happiness.

Diotima: That's right. The reason why happy people are happy is that they have goodness. Love, making all people fascinated, just includes hoping for happiness and goodness. Of course, people, with this desiring, are not all in love. Love and love can't be equated.

Socrates: I am unable to distinguish the difference for a short while.

Diotima: Love includes a variety of desires for happiness. Like poets, athletes, businessmen, they have their own expectations for their respective trades, but this is not the love, only those souls seeking for goodness and beauty can be given the name of love.

Socrates: Yes, I think your view is correct. How does love's devotee usually do in such a pursuit?

Diotima: Love's behavior is the pregnancy of beauty: both in the body and in the soul.

Socrates: I'm worried that this is too esoteric, I can't understand it immediately on the base of my lack of sanity.

Diotima: Yes, I will put it more bluntly. For example, each of us has fertility, while the beauty is goddess dominating inoculation. For those with the sexual maturity, once he or she meets a beautiful lover, soon captivated, inspired, it is easy to pregnancy; if ugly, he or her will be dull, refuse to have sex. Why should we look forward to fertility? Only by reproduction, the lives of ordinary persons can be prolonged and immortal. In other words, sex is hoping for immortality. Love is a road leading to eternity. By love, we feel the existence of goodness and beauty. My dear Socrates, if people's life is worthy of living, it is because we saw beauty itself, rather than confusion by money, handsome boy, beautiful girl, or beautiful clothing. Beauty is eternal.

Socrates:(Applause, clapped along with others) Gentlemen, thank Diotima for wonderful advice, I am convinced. I think you have the same harvest!

Aristophanes: I swear in the name of Dionysus, hopefully Socrates has such a woman!

Socrates: Aristophanes, you satirize others for live, always make fun of me, such an ugly and old man, I always keep indifferent decently for the beauty of the flesh!

Agathon: Haha, my dear Socrates, Aristophanes has been made a fortune by the satirical comedy about you, and you are not unaware of it!

Socrates: Oh, yeah, when watching the "cloud", I rocked with laughter. Aristophanes, you have the right to laugh at everything, you will no doubt be the great father of the comedy in the history of mankind. I swear in the name of Zeus, no matter how you taunt me, I will be your loyal audience. Human laughter is the Gods' gift. In liberal and democratic atmosphere of Athens, there must be citizens' laughter!

Aristophanes: Thank you for Socrates' tolerance and indulgence. Speaking out the truth with a smile is a kind of antidote for people's fanaticism and recalcitrance. However, not everyone can appreciate the true meaning behind the laughter, but some feel angry in the heart only because of its ridicule. Like your tolerance and indulgence, not everyone can do it.   [3]

(Crito comes on the stage.)

Socrates: Crito, how do you come? The discussion we just carried on was very exciting, but unfortunately you missed it.

Crito: I could come early, but just passing through the square, I heard someone spread rumors against you, so I stopped to listen to a few words, and very angry, then I argued with him.

Agathon: Who?

Crito: A man is called Meletus.

Aristophanes: Ha, that crappy poet, I know him. Didn't his speech get the goose?

Crito: On the contrary, he accused you of corroding young people's thought, ungodly.

Phaedo: I've heard of that man, who always spares no effort to oppose you.

Crito: Socrates, I have a proposal that I hope you go somewhere else to take shelter.

Socrates: Leave Athens? It seems that the matter is serious.

 (Aristophanes whistles.)

Crito: Yes. I have a bad sense, some people have always been in opposition to you, and now their influence appears to be growing.

Aristophanes: Socrates, allow me to say seriously. Athens' dignitaries and citizens can bear the "laugh" of my comedy full of laughing and joking, but not necessarily able to tolerate that you endlessly explore the truth.

(Turn to Socrates, and whisper.) I advise you in the name of Dionysus again, be careful, talk much, and errors much, not to be convicted because of speaking. Hopefully you will never receive court summons, and have a calm and happy life. Goodbye! Take care!

Socrates: Thank you for your kindness! I'm not timid and coward. Aristophanes, please remember that courage is to insist on some kind of faith! Friends, goodbye!

(Socrates waves to the crowd, staggering to leave.)

"End"

3

"Act V"

(In Athens' street, some artisans are busy, respectively.)

Shoemaker: He said I was ignorant? I've repaired shoes all my life, who do not know my craft is the most famous in Athens, does he do it?

Pastry Manufacturer: You do not mind what philosopher said.

Carpenter: Sometimes they do not even know what they say.

(Three young onlookers went on, and moved to the artisans.)

Onlooker A: (Pick up a piece of pastry and put it into his mouth, and he says while chewing) Ah, what is it to make you argue fiercely in such a sunny day?

Onlookers B: Must be heatstroke, you should see a doctor.

Onlooker C: In my opinion, they must be pregnant.

Onlooker B: right, right, right, they must be pregnant with the seed of the truth, this is the beginning of philosophy.

Shoemaker: To discuss philosophy should go to find Socrates, who just left, you can catch up.

Onlooker A: Oh? Mr. Socrates has just been here? How could he talk with you?

Onlooker B :(in the face of onlooker C) Yes, they are so ignorant, how could Mr. Socrates talk to them?

Onlooker C: Alas, Mr. Socrates must generously point out their ignorance.

Onlooker A: Alas, Mr. Socrates is really a noble person!

(Young onlookers are talking happily and go off.)

Pastry Manufacturer: Fuck!

Shoemaker: What shameless and arrogant guys!

Carpenter: How have the youth of Athens become like this?

Shoemaker: That's because they were deluded by Socrates!

(Meletus moves to the back area of the stage, and posts a notice on the wall. shoemaker found Meletus. The crowd gathered around gradually.)

Meletus: Athens's citizens, today, here, I, Anytus and Lykon institute legal proceedings against a person. This man claims he is the only who knows he is ignorant. In the face of the young people, he lobbies them by his tongue, and deal in intelligence and wisdom that he thought, pollute young people's mind. The young man, who had committed the sin for Athens Polis, was his student.

(Crito and Phaedo come out of the crowd, Crito stands on a stool.)

Crito: What you said is not true! When that officer went with Socrates together, the teacher's virtues made him able to control of his tendency immorally. But when leaving Socrates, he made friends with some deceptive and blindly fraudulent guys, and some people who make fraudulent; coupled with his origin of eminence, he was seduced and corrupted by many people who were good at flattering, then he ignored self-control. People, like him, can be proud of his origin, and wealth makes them complacent, powers make them arrogant, and many bad guys destroy their virtues, as well as not go with Socrates together for a long time, they become arrogant and willful, is that strange? If they did something wrong, should we blame all of the guilt on Socrates?

Meletus: Oh, really? Not mention he committed a number of atrocities against Athens. Even if your teacher was trying to give a good influence on him, Kritias and Charmides, how do you explain them?

Phaedo: It is not as what you said. My teacher did not agree with what Kritias did, Kritias also hated my teacher. They ordered my teacher......

Carpenter: There must be someone to control them.

Shoemaker: They have to be gave harsh punishment.

Crito: Athens' citizens, don't listen to this man. Do you understand Socrates? Perhaps you have seen Aristophanes' comedy, in which our teacher was described as a man who moved forward in the spiral, claimed that he was able to walk in the air, and talked nonsense. But in fact Socrates is not only a right-minded man, but also a brave man, in our fight against Sparta, he brought the equipment to see action thrice, and very brave. He is loyal to our city-state.

(Phaedo says something to Crito. Phaedo stands on the high platform.)

Meletus: Kritias and Charmides, who were just ousted by us, committed numerous crimes to Athens, their rule were even more cruel that the Spartan's. We don't know how many citizens had been deprived of their lives, and how many people were penniless because of Kritias' misrule, became a beggar in the street from a free citizen. Kritias and Charmides were also his students. I don't know how Mr. Socrates adhering to the principle was to educate these young people. Those who betrayed our country and helped the Spartans were also his students. I don't understand how coincident in the world: those who had been his students all act contrary to their people, all are to hurt their own people again and again.

Phaedo: Citizens, please not follow blindly. Do you remember the trial on Ajiniuse naval battle? All the people insisted killed those generals commanding naval battle, but only Socrates took issue. Facts proved that he was right, that the generals sentenced to death were innocent. He is a man to his own principles.

Meletus: Yes, he adheres to the principle, and he let everyone think they are right. Mr. Anytus, we respected, was penniless after Kritias appeared on the stage, this righteous man wanted his son to inherit his business and continue to develop the family business, but his son was deluded by Socrates, abandoned his own family and responsibilities should be inherited by him, and followed Socrates to boast all day. Citizens, are you willing to see your son use all sorts of words deceitfully to contradict yourself, and only think himself, but neglect his father respectfully, abandon responsibilities for family? Are you willing to see they become like this?

Several people: No! That will be too terrible!

Meletus: And, this man does not fear God, he said the moon is a mass of soil, the sun is a fire. Citizens, it is a man not to respect God! He insists that there is a God in his mind, just listens to its call. My fellow citizens, are you willing to let a man who is godless teach your children all day?

Several people: No!

Carpenter: Now a lot of young people are learning his thoughts, imitating his accent, and made everywhere foul.

Shoemaker: Mr. Meletus, you had better think of a way! If continuing like this, Athens would be finished!

Phaedo: Listen to me, listen to me.

Meletus: So, what do you want me to do?

Shoemaker: Put him out of Athens!

Carpenter and pastry Supplier: right, put him out of Athens! (Meletus make a gesture, and everyone calmed down.)

Meletus: So, I formally charge against Socrates today. We
should let Athens restore strict order, and let everything
restore to its original look.
Crito: We want to plead, plead! Meletus, you wouldn't succeed!
Several people: Let Socrates shut up! Get out of Athens, get
out!

"End"

(Athens court. The trial judge, Socrates, the plaintiff Meletus and so on. Several jurors of the jury, a number of observers. Before the trial, jurors, observers are whispering, talking.)

(A man shouts: "Please be quiet!" The trial judge come out, all stand up. The trial judge has a seat, and all sit down.)

Trial judge: According to Meletus, Anytus and Lykon's allegations, today the trial on Socrates is officially launched. According to the plaintiff's allegations, Socrates committed the offenses as follows: the commitment of heresy, instigate others to learn from him, the expression of the wrong idea to young people, corrupt the youths' minds. Tribunal of First Instance is that Socrates is convicted, now Socrates defends for himself and asked the jury to make a ruling.

Socrates: Gentlemen, I am seventy years, and this is the first time for me to stand on the court, so I don't know how to speak. If there are inappropriate parts, please forgive me. Gentlemen, I don't know what effect the plaintiff has on you, but for me, I'm going to be mad by them. The plaintiffs have complained me for many years. Since I am taking a dismissive attitude, because of jealousy and liking slander, these people want to incite you against me, and to kill me with the law. These are a group of extremely brazen and ferocious people!

Judge: Please pay attention to your words!

Socrates: Well, Mr. Judge. I have to try to defend myself in accordance with the law in the short time the court specified. I quite know I am in dangerous situation currently. They accused me of corrupting the youths and impiety in the proceedings. In Aristophanes' play you have seen, that man, who was called Socrates, claimed himself to be able to walk in the air, talking nonsense seemingly with a high fever. You all know me, and heard what I usually said, how can you believe a dramatist's fictional image on the stage and convict me by this?

Aristophanes: I protest, you can't use play I fabricated as evidence!

A person :(Shout) Aristophanes, if Socrates was honest, well-behaved, you couldn't write a drama to satire Socrates! No smoke without fire!

(Aristophanes wants to say something, but blocked by Socrates.)

Socrates: Yes, I see this gentleman. On this point, it was a long story. Gentlemen, the reason I got this reputation is simply because I have some wisdom.

A person :(Shout) You are boasting!

Socrates: Gentlemen, I seemed to talk wildly. Please not interrupt me, I want to tell you that these words are not of my own views, but the order of the sun and the god of wisdom, God will testify to my wisdom.

Judge: Socrates, please not digress!

Socrates: Okay, Mr. Judge, I make it short. You certainly know Kettler, who is my friend since childhood, and also an outstanding democrat, not long ago, he was banished. You know what he is. He is very enthusiastic when working. Once, he even went to Delphi Temple, and asked the Apollo's for advice.

Someone in the public gallery: (Shout) Baloney!

Socrates: Please not interrupt me, let me finish! He asked God: "Who is smarter than Socrates in this world?" God replied:

"No." Kettler has been dead, but his brother sits on the court at the moment, who can testify for me words. This is the fundamental reason that they attack me. Listen to this oracle, I can't believe it. I am very clear that I don't have any wisdom, but why did God say that I was the most intelligent people in the world? God can't lie, otherwise it would not match its nature!

Judge: God can't lie, but maybe you can.

Socrates: Yes, I have the same question, and have confused for a long time, so I decided to test the true meaning of the oracle. I went to visit a man who had a high wisdom and prestige, and I believed he must be smarter than me, in this way, the oracle would prove unfounded. So I conducted the investigation for him completely. He was an outstanding statesman. However, the result made me disappointed. He looked very smart, but in fact not smart. When I told him frankly, he produced resentment. Then I went to visit another wise man with greater reputation, the results I got the same impression, and I offended him as well. So, since then, I have visited and asked for advice one by one, the results were the same, they thought I was arrogant, more and more hated me.

Meletus: He is so annoying that he should be put to death.

Socrates: The oracle has been testified, but my surveys have made me pounded on all sides, extremely vicious and stubborn slander. Many rich young men saw me ask a lot of people for questions, and then they also imitated me to ask others, as a result, people questioned didn't hate them, but blamed me. They complained that there was a busy man, spreading plague, called Socrates, who expressed the wrong idea to the youth. If you ask them what Socrates did in the end, they could not point. Just as Meletus yelling to execute me here just now, considering himself as the patriot with a high degree of conscience, accusing me of committing a crime of corrupting the youth. So, come on, Meletus, do you think our youths should have a good education?

Meletus: Yes.

Socrates: Very good. So, please tell us, who can make them get a good education?

Meletus: It's, it's, it's...... (prevarication, he could not answer it)

Socrates: You see, Meletus, your tongue was tied. What a shame, my friend! Please tell me, who is making the youth learn well?

Meletus: It's legal!

Socrates: My dear sir, so, who knows the law?

Meletus: Here gentlemen, members of the jury.

Socrates: You mean they have the ability to educate young people well?

Meletus: Of course!

Socrates: all understanding the law can make young people learn well, or only certain judges can educate young people well?

Meletus: All the judges.

Socrates: Great! In the world there are so many people able to make the youth to learn well. Then, do these listeners on the court make the youths learn well, either?

Meletus: Yes, they can educate the youths well.

Socrates: The others? Meletus, is it all the Athenians that could educate the youths well?

Meletus: Yes.

Socrates: In this case, all the citizens of Athens are making

the youths learn well, only I, Socrates corrupts the youths.
Is that what you mean?

Meletus: Yes, exactly what I mean. The wicked has a bad effect
on their intimate friends, the good guy has on a good impact,
right?

Socrates: Do you think anyone would deliberately go together
with the bad guys and suffer from the injury?

Meletus: Of course not!

Socrates: Why do I misguide others and then let them harm me?
Answer me! The law requires you to answer!

Meletus: (Stunned for a moment) You incite them to believe
the new God, rather than believe the gods recognized by the
State.

Socrates: Do you accuse me in the end of abetting others to
believe in the new god, or not believing in any Gods and
abetting others to do the same?

Meletus: I say you totally do not believe in God.

Socrates: But you really surprised me, Meletus, if you say
that, what purpose is it? Do you mean I don't believe that
the sun and moon is God like others?

Meletus: Yes, gentlemen of the jury, Socrates doesn't
certainly believe in God, because he said the sun was a fire,
the moon is a mass of soil.

Socrates: Dear Meletus, don't you think you are being accusing
Anaxagoras, right? You can buy a book with a bit of money,
to look. The contents were written in there by him.

Meletus: I don't believe that, absolutely not!

Socrates: Meletus, there is a kind of person in the world:
he believes in human activities, but not believe the existence
of human being, is there such people? Let Meletus answer

questions, gentlemen, don't let him say "opposition".

Meletus: No.

Socrates: Great! Under the force of the court, you finally speak out a word. I would like to ask, the supernatural beings are treated as gods' children, do you agree?

Meletus: Yes.

Socrates: I say I believe in the supernatural activity, do you agree?

Meletus: Certainly I agree.

Socrates: I believe in supernatural activity, but not believe in supernatural beings? I think you test my intelligence in order to fun. In this world, who could believe there were the gods' children, rather than believe in the gods? This is just as ridiculous as you believe there is a foal but not believe there is a horse. Meletus, you use the lack of faith to accuse me, maybe test my wisdom by this, maybe you simply can't find the real guilt to sue me.

In fact, for Meletus' charge, I don't need to do more to defend myself. If anything happens, then it will be not today's trial to work, but all people's lies and jealousy. I shouldn't appear on this court, but I have been in the court now, you must execute me, because if I escaped, your sons would go to practice Socrates' teachings at once, and completely degenerate. If you are willing to give mercy, let me leave, there would be certainly be a condition that is to require me to give up the exploration of the wisdom and stop working on philosophy.

I'll answer like this: As long as I have life and ability, I will never stop the practice of philosophy, and clarify the truth to everyone I met. I will continue to say by the usual way, my friend, you are an Athenian, part of the city known to the world because of the wisdom and strength.

Phaedo: Well done, teacher!

Crowd: Well done!

Crowd: Wonderful!

Crowd: You will be not guilty.

Judge: The defendant's plea is over.

(Meletus puts his hand, steps forward.)

Meletus: My fellow citizens, I would like to reiterate that, if we want to restore order of Athens, we should punish Socrates severely, otherwise, he would therefore become more arrogant. I reiterate again, and hope citizens carefully cast your vote. Your vote will decide the future of Athens.

Judge: Now please plaintiff and defendant give advice for sentencing. Mr. Meletus?

Meletus: Death penalty.

Judge: Mr. Socrates?

Koscipa: Wait, Mr. Judge, I was Socrates' wife, I ask for saying a few words.

Judge: Okay.

G Shan SIPA: Socrates, listen to me, to pray for judge, we can accept the penalty, no matter how much money it is, I can go to borrow. Beg the judge to give you a light sentence, even if exile, where you go, I will take our sons to follow you.

(The sound of the erhu starts.)

Crito: Teacher, we can accept the penalty, no matter how much money it is, we cǎn afford it, many people are willing to pay the money for you.

(Socrates keeps silent for a long time.)

Judge: now defendant gives advice for sentencing. Mr. Socrates?

Socrates: Gentlemen, I have to quite cherish my life so that I will accept exile, forced to move from one city to another city, and seen off each time, but for my age, I'm afraid that it would be difficult for me to live such a life. In addition, I am not used fine, because I have no money, I can only pay one hundred drachmas.

Koscipa: No, Socrates! We can pay more.

(Crito gave a sign to Socrates.)

Socrates: Gentlemen, wait, Crito, sitting over there, wants me to increase the fine to three thousand drachmas, I agree, at the same time, you can believe these gentlemen will pay.

Judge: Now Socrates's sentencing is the death penalty and a fine of three thousand drachmas. Please citizens vote.

"End"

3

"Act VII"

(Special lighting effects, chorus, voting, accompanied by music, were ritualistically carried out.)

(The scene is the same as the former. Socrates' case entered final judgment. The observers and jurors were talking about it. A man shouted "keep silent". (The presiding judge and other judges come to the count, and all stand up, then sit down.)
Presiding judge: Now open a court session. After the jury's voting, a total of 281 votes supported the guilty of Socrates, 220 votes opposed the guilty of Socrates. According to the principle of majority, I now make a judgment: sentence Socrates to death. He will be executed next day.

(The court is in tumult. Applause, cheering, screaming, crying ......)
Presiding judge: Quiet, be quiet, please keep order! (It is silent later) Now, please Socrates makes a final statement.
Socrates :(Stood up slowly and looked around) Gentlemen, I have had to defense myself twice according to the law, you've already known the truth. I am well aware that my truth makes you resentment and disgust, which proves that what I talked is the truth. That I was put to death is not because of lack of evidence, but the lack of audacity and cowardice. In fact, I refuse to speak by the way you like. You like to see me cry, hear me put myself worthless, and you are accustomed to hearing such words from others.
Someone: Wronged!
Someone: Bullshit, let her shut up!
Socrates: Gentlemen, for the final judgment, I don't feel frustrated. It is expected. If I spend more money, I can be

exempted from the death completely, but I don't want to do that. I am not interested in making money, working in government, and having a luxury live like most people. I consider myself really straightforward, even silly, and try to persuade everyone not to care about the material benefits more than the spirit and moral. By rights, my upright should get the national award. So, if there is a bit of fair, the appropriate punishment for me should be that the country supports money for me, enough to live comfortably.

A jury: Haha, he is really daydreaming!

(There is some buzz in the audience.)

Socrates: In the past, when I was a soldier, my comrades and I risked our lives to our posts together. Then I obeyed God's command, began to have a life of philosophy, for myself and others to observe and think, I can't abandon my duty and mission because of fear of death or other dangers. If I can't stick to it consistently, then I would not be Socrates.

(There are arguments on the court.)

Socrates: Please be quiet, gentlemen, listen to me! Fear of death is just another kind of ignorance, perhaps for people the death is a kind of the greatest happiness. But people are afraid of death, as if they can be sure that death is the greatest evil, like this ignorance, it is typically of pretending to understand, and it should be the ignorance punished most.

(There are arguments on the court.)

Presiding Judge: Please keep quiet.

Socrates: Dear, Mr. Judges, I call you, because I hope you are worthy of this title. There have been many innocent people framed, and I think this situation will continue. You are

bringing an innocent man to death, which will be a catastrophe
for democracy and law. My death will be a great irony for the
democratic politics of Athens, which will be a taint that it
couldn't get rid of forever, you think about it, how will be
evaluated in history?

Koscipa:(Crying) Socrates, my dear, for my sake, please you
don't keep saying, you beg the judges!

Socrates: Mr. Judge, please bring her out of the courtroom.
She is my wife, and I wouldn't let her get hurt.

Presiding judge: It's her freedom, and I have no right to
interfere. Do you still have relations?

Socrates: Dear sir, of course, I have! With Homer's words,
I didn't jump out from rocks or old oak. Gentlemen, I have
three sons. One is close to an adult, and the other two are
still very little, but that won't the reason that I beg you.

Presiding Judge: Well, Socrates, you will be in the face of
the death alone!

Socrates: Kill me! Let me make predictions for your fates.
I want to tell you, if I die, the revenge will happen to you,
and you will suffer from more painful punishment than you kill
me. You will be subject to more criticism, and the youths
criticizing you will treat you more harshly, make you more
embarrassed. If you expect to criticize wrong way to live by
the way to execute people, then you are wrong. This way to
escape is neither possible, nor credible. The best way is not
to keep others' mouth close, but you should try your best to
do good deeds. I very understand I'd better die. It's time
for me to get rid of the upset. It should be over, I'm going
to die, and you are going to live, which is more happiness?
Only God knows!

Someone: Well done!

Someone: let him shut up. It's an arrogant man!

Someone: Shut up!

Someone: Take him away!

Someone: An arrogant man. Death is at hand, what else you can say!

Someone: Let you, this ignorant and clever man, die!

(All sounds were louder and louder, and finally, Socrates was overwhelmed completely.)

Presiding Judge: Now, take Socrates into death row, retire!

"End"

3

"Act Ⅷ "

(The music starts first, there is a dim lamp. Socrates is in the prison alone, wearing handcuffs and leg irons, thinking about something.)

(A jailer came on the stage, Aristophanes and others were outside the prison door. The jailer took off Socrates' handcuffs and leg irons, and gave a sign to Aristophanes to come in. Aristophanes came on the stage, and the jailer went away. Aristophanes looked around in the prison.)

Aristophanes: God said Sophocles was smart, and Euripides was smarter, but Socrates was the smartest. I didn't expect the reason I first went to jail was actually to visit the smartest people in the world.

Socrates: Oh, dear Aristophanes, please don't have a prejudice against the prison. In fact, the prison is not a bad place.

Aristophanes: So, the next time I must write a play happening in the prison.

Socrates: This bed will empty out tonight, you'd better move over here to stay.

Aristophanes: I'd like to sleep here after you, but unfortunately I don't have this opportunity, there are not so many people hating me. I'm a writer of comedy, my creation can make people happy, and make myself painful, but you're a philosopher, your thoughts can make yourself happy, but make others pain.

Socrates: Compared to serious thoughts, Athenians obviously feel like the cheap laugh better. However, in fact, the philosopher can do a lot except making people painful. For example, he will make people laugh when appearing in comedy, just as I appear in your drama.

Aristophanes: My friend, you should know that I was in the creation of the "cloud" when I was not...... I didn't think of......

Socrates: Take it easy, my friend, I don't want to blame you, on the contrary, I think "cloud" is a very good work. As what I said, ridicule is the test of the truth, and it is a corrective force to prevent us from absurd.

(A long silence.)

Aristophanes: Then I said I should take care, or "loose lips sink ships", I can't be convicted of words.

Socrates: So, you were still a prophet.

Aristophanes: If I was really a prophet, I'd want to be able to take the first prize in the Dionysia theater competition before leaving the world.

Socrates: I guess I can't do the judge of the Dionysia this year, maybe you have the chance.

(Aristophanes and Socrates continues laughing. The jailer opens the cell door, and Crito came in, turned round and gave the jailer some money. The jailer leaves.)

Crito: Socrates, you make me so surprised. You are actually laughing. I've been feeling your mind was cheerful and stretch, but now that I don't expect, facing imminent catastrophe, you are still calm, I really admire you so much.

Socrates: Frankly speaking, Crito, if I still feared of death at my ages, then[3] it would be too absurd.

Crito: But, Socrates, if those people with the same age as yours encounter this situation, can they do like you? I think, certainly not. Who is afraid of death?

Socrates: You are right. But, you are here, don't want to say words like these, right?

Crito : (keep silent for a moment) Socrates, I got a bad news, I'm so sorry.

Socrates: (laugh with Aristophane) I've known it.

Crito : (slightly hesitant) Socrates, today ...... today, you would be killed certainly.

Socrates: Well, Crito, don't be sad. I've been looking forward to this outcome.

Crito: Why, Socrates? But now, you can accept my suggestion, it is not too late to run away. If you died, not only I would therefore lose a friend who can't be replaced forever, and would also be reviled as an unjust and heartless man, because I have the ability to save you to go out, but I don't. As long as they can be bribed by money, it would be very easy. If I tell them that you would rather be killed than refuse to be rescued, who would believe it?

Socrates: My dear Crito, why do you think what others think of it?

Crito: you can think according to your thoughts, Socrates, do you think your escape would make us in trouble, don't you? If you have such scruples, then put it to scrap! You accept my suggestion, don't be stubborn!

Socrates: I totally understand what you said, Crito, I'm not worried about these.

Crito: So, don't hesitate! I know some people, they are willing to pay for rescuing you to go out here, and send you out of this country. In addition, I've prepared a lot of money for you, which will afford your life. If you're worried about my safety, and wouldn't like to spend my money, then I tell you, those Gentiles who live in Athens are also willing to contribute generously. There are a few people who have given the money. So I think, you don't think blindly, and don't think twice what you said in court. Besides, Socrates, I don't think your approach is right, why did you give it up when you were able to save your own live? Your enemies let you die, would you die? Don't you help the enemy? Not only you destroy yourself, but also destroy your sons. You think how many difficulties orphans who lose their parents will encounter. You really make me feel weird, even pedantic. Oh, my god, how can we fall on this point? Now we can escape, but you are indifferent. It is indeed not too late. Make up your mind, Socrates, don't be stubborn please!

Socrates: Dear Crito, I am very grateful to your truths, that is, I assume these truths have some justification, otherwise......

Crito :(Interrupt) I will listen to your tirade after you escape. I am so worried!

Socrates: Well, how can we consider this problem rationally? Suppose we should go back to your viewpoints on public opinion.

Crito: Well, Socrates, there is no time. You are still talking about rationality? Give a final decision!

Socrates: I believe that serious thinkers always have the viewpoints that I mentioned......

Crito: right, right, you are right! What should we do, run or not run in the end?

Socrates: Crito, you tell me, is a person going to harm others?

Crito: Of course not, Socrates.

Socrates: So, is it right to hurt others for revenge? Most people think it is right.

Crito: No, it's not right.

Socrates: So, for whatever reason, a man shouldn't be to revenge, an eye for an eye.

Crito: I agree with you. I also hold it.

Socrates: So, please consider the logical conclusion. If we don't obtain the prior consent of the State and leave here without authorization, then can't we harm our country, and revenge for the irrational behavior by means of damage? Just because of an unfair trial I suffered.

Crito: I can't answer your question, Socrates, my mind has been in turmoil.

Socrates: Suppose we are going to escape from here, I would be queried by Athens' law: "Socrates, do you want to take action to destroy our law? What you are against us and the state in the name of? Such a principle has been reached between you and our law: any Athenians, to adulthood, recognize the country's political organization and law, if he feels dissatisfied, then we will allow him to bring the property to move to any place. If you are dissatisfied with us, in your seventy-year career, you can be ready to leave the country at any time. If you don't choose other Greek city-states or overseas cities, then we think you agree with this contract. Furthermore, in the trial, if you choose exile, and get permission, then you can leave now. But, then you didn't care about whether you would be killed, showing a noble image, and now you don't follow the declaration earlier, don't respect our laws, attempt to escape. You were simply the most humble people due to your act. Now I ask you, if you violate your own guarantee and declarations? "Crito, if I ran away, wouldn't I break my promise?

Crito: Yes, Socrates.

Socrates: The law will continue to say: "Is there no one to accuse you? Like you, an old man, last days are numbered, would you like to violate the majesty of law by all means, so greedily to grab a slim chance of survival yet? We should like to know, where do your good and honest arguments go? If you run away, you and your friends will thus be in trouble, because you lose integrity, and tarnish the purity of conscience. When you went to another world, you wouldn't get good karma. If you revenge, sin for sin, to escape from this place, and destroy our contract we made, then you will hurt yourself, your friends, your country and our laws. Crito, my dear friend, I tell you solemnly that I seem to get advice of law, just as I heard the voice of God. I believe my idea is correct. But if you think you can persuade me, please speak,

Crito: no, Socrates, I have nothing to say.

Socrates: Well, Crito, since God has pointed out the way, let us follow God's will to act!

(Koscipa, Socrates' sons and Phaedo come on the stage. His sons throw themselves on Socrates, and Koscipa walks over to sit beside the bed.)

Koscipa: The boat, to Delos, is coming back today, I heard.

Socrates: Crito, Phaedo will take good care of you.

(Phaedo and Crito left, and Aristophanes led Socrates Sons to move aside.)

Koscipa: Oh, Socrates, this is my last visit to you? Gee, how about my kids and me!

Socrates: My dear wife, don't cry, sooner or later this day would come, you shouldn't show a woman's cowardice to our kids, don't scare them.

Koscipa: Oh, Socrates, this is your last time to converse with your friends.

Socrates: Yes.

(Koscipa snuggled up to Socrates, Meletus appeared, and met with

Phaedo and Crito.)

Crito: You are to oversee Socrates, right? Sorry, I disappoint you! I've done everything I can to persuade the teacher and told him that a lot of people hoped to pick him up, but the teacher was unmoved.

Meletus: As the enemy, I admire Socrates.

Phaedo: as an enemy against Socrates, you are not eligible.

Meletus: Maybe in your eyes I am a scumbag, but as far as I uphold the belief, I have a clear conscience.

Phaedo: If you really have a clear conscience, why do you come here full of sorrow and tears?

Meletus: Maybe you don't believe what I will say. But I am still going to say that I admire Socrates in my heart. His courage, fearless. I thought to myself there is no such quality, and I feel ashamed.

Phaedo: Please get out here. Sadness can't scrub the stain on your conscience, at least for now, at this moment of sorrow. Please go, let Socrates leave quietly.

(Meletus left, the Phaedo and Crito returned to the house.)

Koscipa: (Crying) Socrates......

Socrates: Don't be crying. Death is a part of life. I have a clear conscience, which is is innocence, I will be happy to exist in that world. Go home, look after our sons.

 (Koscipa and his sons left.)

Socrates: Suddenly I remembered lovely Plato, where he is?

Phaedo: Mr. Socrates, according to your teachings, Plato is studying in another city, who don't know what happens to you.

Socrates: Oh, I think of it. Please tell Plato, let him take advantage of the young to study all around, can't be limited to Athens. Read more books, practice, not thinking, but also listening, to learn widely from others' strong points, in order to make your way in life.

Phaedo: Well, I must convey your teachings to Plato.

(The jailer appears.)

Jailer: Socrates, time is up. I'm the bailiff. Anyway, if you are angry and curse me like everyone else when I let them drink poison, I don't think you have anything wrong. I've already known you're the noblest, bravest, decent man among all the people coming here. So, now you know what I'll say, goodbye. If you can make yourself easy to suffer, then you just do it.

Socrates: Goodbye. I will do as what you said.

(The jailer leave.)

Socrates: In fact, he is a good guy! When I stayed here he was always taking care of me, sometimes he still discussed the issues with me, and showed great concern with me. He was so kind, and now actually shed tears for me! Come on, Crito, let us do as what he said. If the poison is prepared, you go to find someone to bring the poison; If not, tell that person to prepare quickly.

Crito: Socrates, now the sun is definitely still above the top of the hill. It's still early. So, we don't need to hurry. We also have ample time.

Socrates: Early to drink, early to leave. There is no need to dawdle. Since I drink it later, I can't get anything, instead, make myself get quite ridiculous. Follow what I said.

(The bailiff holds a glass of poisoned wine prepared.)

Socrates: Oh, my good fellow, you know these things, how can I do?

Bailiff: Just drink it, then stand up and walk until your legs feel heavy, at that time, to lie down. Poison itself will work.

(Socrates takes over the glass.)

Socrates: Can I sprinkle a little on the ground to sacrifice Gods? May I?

Bailiff: We only have the preparation of a normal dose that we think.

Socrates: I know, but I guess I should be allowed or pray to the gods, I hope I understand this world and enter into another world full of happiness to continue to think by my philosophy. This is my prayer.

 (Socrates drinks up the poison. The people around him begin to sob.)

Socrates: Honestly, my friends, don't cry to see me off. That is the main reason I sent away the woman. With the last breath, he should keep a quiet mood. You should calm and get strong.

(Socrates walks for a while, and then sits on the bed.)

Socrates: I think my legs feel heavy.

(Socrates lays down. The supervisor checks Socrates' legs)

Bailiff: Have a feeling?

Socrates: no feeling, no feeling.

(Silent.)

Socrates: Crito, [3]remember to offer a cock to Death, to thank him for making my life complete with death.

Crito:I can't forget. I will do it.

(Silence.)

The music starts, everyone enters from all directions, Crito, Phaedo and Aristophanes hold Socrates to walk upward, everyone stops, watching a few people carrying Socrates to disappear.

Voiceover:

1. The nature of moderation is to understand itself.

2. A true philosopher can die for the faith, and death is not enough to cause their fear.

3. Wisdom can make people lucky anywhere.

4. There is no evil man, which will the happiest in souls' world.

5. It is a fraud if all knowledge digresses from virtue and justice.

6. A right decision isn't related to the number of people.

7. ...... Really important thing is not to live, but live ......

I

"End"

3